Lilian Whiting

After her Death

The Story of a Summer

Lilian Whiting

After her Death
The Story of a Summer

ISBN/EAN: 9783337404949

Printed in Europe, USA, Canada, Australia, Japan

Cover: Foto ©Andreas Hilbeck / pixelio.de

More available books at **www.hansebooks.com**

AFTER HER DEATH

The Story of a Summer

BY THE AUTHOR OF

"THE WORLD BEAUTIFUL" (FIRST AND SECOND SERIES)
AND "FROM DREAMLAND SENT"

"The eager fate that carried thee
Took the largest part of me"

BOSTON
ROBERTS BROTHERS
1897

TO

ONE WHOSE PRESENCE IN THE SEEN OR IN THE
UNSEEN WOULD EVER MAKE FOR ME
A "WORLD BEAUTIFUL,"

This Little Story

OF THE SUMMER AFTER HER DEATH
IS TENDERLY INSCRIBED.

"And she the rest will comprehend, will comprehend"

CONTENTS.

WHAT LACKS THE SUMMER?

What lacks the Summer?
           O light and savor,
  And message of healing the world above!
Gone is the old-time strength and flavor,
  Gone is its old-time peace and love!
Gone is the bloom of the shimmering meadow,
  Music of birds, as they sweep and fall, —
All the great world is dim with shadow,
  Because no longer mine eyes can see
  The eyes that made Summer and life for me, —
      And that is all.

                  MARY ELIZABETH BLAKE.

AFTER HER DEATH.

WHAT LACKS THE SUMMER?

"Star to star vibrates light! may soul to soul
Strike through a finer element of her own?"

OUR friendship had always seemed to me one made for heaven rather than for earth; as of a nature adapted to different conditions from those ordinarily prevailing here; and after the first bewildering agony — caused by the tidings of her death — was over, I began to realize how that subtle and curiously insistent telepathic communion between us seemed to adjust itself anew and became more clear and intense. But, ah, that first flash of bewildering pain! Will even eternity be long enough for its remembrance ever to be dimmed?

It was a June morning in Paris. For two weeks preceding I had been so strangely sad, so desolate and distraught that the days were a problem to me. And why? I could not imagine. Some three weeks previous I had fared forth on that first voyage to foreign lands which always prefigures itself in life as an experience that can never be repeated. Other visits may be as happy, or happier; but there is a thrill in one's first glimpse of Europe that — as Mr. Stoddard sings of that indescribable sensation that "follows youth with flying feet" — is one that "never comes again," whatever better and finer things, perchance, may come. The voyage had been an ideal one, full, to me, of a curious uplift of feeling that suddenly changed, the day we landed, to a sadness and desolation inexpressible, and for which no adequate cause could be even faintly conjectured. No letters or cablegram of depressing nature had reached me; and still, on landing at Liverpool after the happy voyage on the good steamer "Pavonia," I was absolutely unable to fulfil a previously arranged programme of proceeding to London by a détour to Stratford-on-Avon and Oxford, with leisurely loitering, and could only take the first train to the great metropolis, trusting that its rush of life might exorcise the strange spell that was flung over me.

This swift change of feeling from exhilaration of spirits to an unutterable desolation was initiated by an experience for which I can suggest no explanation; but the occurrence was one which leaves an impress that will forever stand as a crisis hour in life. It was this.

On our last night on shipboard we had enjoyed the usual merry time of the " Captain's dinner " with its gala and laughter, and had retired with the happy anticipations of landing at Liverpool in the early morning. I had been asleep for some hours when, suddenly, as if by an electric shock, I found myself standing on the floor of my stateroom, with the quiver of a current of electricity pervading me from head to feet as if I grasped a strongly charged battery. I turned on the electric light and looked at my watch. It was nearly four in

the morning. The words I had just heard —
not with the outer ear, but with some inner
sense — vibrated in the air. For I had seemed
to see standing, I knew not where, three forms,
which, by the same inexplicable inner sense, I
knew were in the ethereal, not the natural,
world: I seemed, too, to know that one of
these had but just entered that world, and I
heard her say, in tones of mingled joy, amazement, incredulity, and triumph, "Is *this* all?
It is all over!"

Then I said to myself: "Some one I know
has just died, — some one whose death will
make the greatest difference to me." Yet,
strangely, I did not think of *her*, — in whose
presence or absence the entire world always
changed to me, — she with whom I constantly
lived in thought, whether we were together
or whether half the world stretched its space
between us. If this were a creation of fiction
and not a narration of actual fact, I should
record that my first thought was of her; that
I recognized it was her voice that thrilled
through my dreams, and startled me, with a

force that fairly shot me from a sound slumber
to find myself standing, — it would be a more
rhythmic sequence; but this is not an imaginative tale : it is the record of an actual experience. I did not think of her, and it could
almost be added that it was the only moment
since I had known the happiness of meeting her
that she was not in my thoughts. Almost at
once, too, I again fell into a deep sleep, which
was incongruous with the startled shock, and
slept so soundly that the pretty stewardess was
quite discouraged in her attempts to induce me
to rise at the necessary hour for leaving the ship.
But on awakening in the morning that dread
desolation, unanalyzed and unaccountable, set-
tled down over me. Had I been shipwrecked
and left alone on an island in the sea, I could
not have been more — and I fancy I should
have been less — desolate. For it is invariably true that when all of the visible fails us,
the invisible is potent to protect and comfort.
It was in vain that I attempted to combat
this apparently idle depression. It could not
be reasoned away ; but, as I said, it was so

overpowering that I abandoned perforce the anticipated tour to the home and haunts of the bard of Avon, and the visit to classic Oxford, which had been one of the most prized anticipations, and went directly to London.

Still, the sense of unutterable desolation persisted, and the six weeks planned for London were reduced to six days, when, in a kind of desperate attempt to break the spell, I departed for Paris. While in London nothing had so enchained me as the stately, solemn beauty of Westminster Abbey. And perhaps the most impressive thing in the old abbey was not the majesty of sculptured marbles, or even the marvellous magnificence of the Chapel of Henry VII., but, instead, the little old Chapel of St. Faith. It is a very small one, of rude stone, — ceiling, walls, and floor, — lying between the chapter-house and the south transept. Over the old altar is a faded picture in which one dimly traces the outline of St. Faith above the crucifixion. On the table below are a crucifix and two tall candles, and on the altar a Latin inscription which runs, in translation : —

"From the burden of my sore transgression, sweet Virgin, deliver me: make my peace with God and blot out mine offence."

An inscription at the entrance enjoins that no word shall ever be spoken within it; that it shall be kept solely for silent prayer. A tablet on one wall records that by the wish of Dean Stanley the body of Bishop McIlvaine of Ohio rested in this chapel during the journey from Florence to the United States, and that his life and work "helped to draw together England and America in one communion of faith and love." Something in the atmosphere of the place sustained and soothed me in an exceptional way, and I found myself daily kneeling at the old altar in the silence, with perpetual prayer and thought for *her*, though I did not realize that there was hardly more than the usual tender turning to her, and perhaps there was not. All my life, so to speak, had been so magnetized toward her that this feeling could only increase with the increased fulness and depth of years.

For our friendship, on my part, had really

2

begun long years before she dawned upon my
vision. She was so richly endowed that even
in her earliest youth her powers expressed
themselves in a way that the fame of a great
and gifted woman crowned her radiant girlhood. Taken as a young girl to Florence,
where she studied music under Garcia ; where
the poet Landor taught her Latin, and himself
wrote verses to her ; where she studied the
languages, and met and loved Mrs. Browning,
who often kept the gifted girl for days as her
guest at Casa Guidi, — here in Florence she
found her native air of art and inspiration. It
was the atmosphere to which she was born, and
it was a part of the divine destiny of her noble
life that in her beautiful youth she should
have come under these marvellous influences.
It was here she met George Eliot, who was
strongly attracted by the brilliant girl, and who
gave her wise counsel and strong stimulus.

Her rich gifts and these felicitous circumstances conspired to allow her to win early
fame in the world of letters ; and while I was
still a child, treading the quiet ways of a coun-

try home, her literary work touched the spring
of enthusiasm, and I learned to watch for it
and love it until it became the central interest
in my life. My day-dreams were of her,
this radiant figure out in an unknown and
enchanted world, — Florence and Rome and
Paris; and at night I would lie awake, wish-
ing that by some magic her picture would
flash upon me through the darkness. The
years sped on, and she dominated my girlhood.
To my girlish fancy, as later to the perception
of my womanhood, she seemed to impersonate
the genius of nobleness.

It must have been a dozen years that I thus
thought of her and dreamed of her afar, before
the inscrutable ways of destiny at last brought
me within the horizon of her life; and from
the hour of our first meeting the hope to so
live as to grow less and less unworthy to be
her friend became to me the dominant note
in life. Nor was it a narrow, human limitation. For I could not but recognize — though
far too feebly and too crudely — how great
was the quality of her spirit.

     " 'T is human fortune's happiest height to be
     A spirit melodious, lucid, poised, and whole :
     Second, in order of felicity,
     I hold it, to have walked with such a soul."

And so, long before we met in the visible world, the spiritual link was forged which finally drew me to her on earth, and which, let me reverently trust, will ere long bring me again to that dear presence by which all my days and dreams are still companioned. The entire story of our friendship is simply a story of spiritual destiny. I always saw her, not in the mere visible and tangible setting and scenery of the moment, but in what I may perhaps venture to term the ethereal atmosphere, — in a world partly denoted in these lines of a little Impromptu that I once wrote to her, though it was afterward published under a veiled title. The lines ran : —

    I do not find you in the outer life.
    Always I see you in those gardens fair
    With starry jasmine shining in your hair,
    Apart from noise and fret of daily life
    With which the day and daylight world are rife.
    Always I see you, Love, in regions where
    Immortal Landor trod, great spirits came,

Whose fire of genius set your own aflame,
Your girlish voice inspiring loud acclaim.
Always I see you in those gardens where
Music and fragrance linger on the air ;
Where she " who sang of Italy " still lies
Beneath the glory of the starlit skies,
Whose beauty held her in a glad surprise.
Flower of all Cities ! City of all Flowers !
'T is there you linger in the charmèd hours ;
With jasmine in your hair I see you stand
Fair in the grace of that Enchanted Land.

And so it was that our friendship always seemed to me as made for heaven rather than for earth ; and so it is that since she has entered into the invisible world it has assumed a power and a proportion and an unmistakable and marvellous influence over events which must be my explanation of the little record of this story. For the time has now come, in the evolution of social progress, when all that tends to throw any light upon the real relations between the Seen and the Unseen is of common interest to us all, and in mutual comparison of experiences we may hope to evolve actual knowledge of the conditions of the life just beyond the present.

FROM INMOST DREAMLAND.

Thy voice from inmost dreamland calls;
　The wastes of sleep thou makest fair;
Bright o'er the ridge of darkness falls
　The cataract of thy hair.

The morn renews its golden birth;
　Thou with the vanquished night dost fade,
And leav'st the ponderable earth
　Less real than thy shade.

WILLIAM WATSON.

FROM INMOST DREAMLAND.

"Less yearning for the friendship fled
Than some strong bond which is to be."

S I have said, I had long had a girl's dreams of her as an enchanting figure out in a gay, glad world yet unrevealed to me. It was as vague and unreal as the ethereal world can seem to any one here amid the things of sense. When, at last, I came within the charmed circle of her life, she became to me the magnetic centre. So that when, on that June day in Paris, as the sunny radiance of the morning flooded the Champs Élysées with balm and bloom and radiant energy, I learned from a cablegram that she had already been for more than two weeks in the life beyond; that her death had occurred the very day that I landed at Liverpool and had been given that thrilling

vision of my last night on the steamer; when
I realized that her death occurred on that far
away island in the Pacific where there is no
cable communication, and that it had taken
the two weeks for the tidings to reach the
United States, — in that first moment of blind,
bewildering agony there was little of conscious
reflection or thought.   The morning was as fair
as a dream of Paradise.   The song of birds came
from the leafy foliage in the Champs Élysées.
The crystal play of the fountains in the Place
de la Concorde gleamed in a thousand iri-
descent hues in the golden sunshine.   The
little garden into which I wandered was fra-
grant with blossoms.

And *she* had gone!

> " Oh, alone, alone, —
> Not troubling any in heaven, or any on earth, —
> I stood there in the garden and looked up
> The deaf blue sky that brings the roses out
> On such June mornings."

Reading time backward, like the Chaldeans,
many things began to grow clear.   The voice
and the vision that thrilled me like a strong

current of electricity, in that last night on the "Pavonia," were now explained. It was *she* whom I had seen as she entered the unknown world; it was *her* voice that I had heard in that tone of mingled amazement, incredulity, and exaltation. There was to me a solemn impressiveness in this which seemed, in that moment of supremest pain, to say, "Be still, and know that I am God."

On this day there began for me a summer of either very curious coincidences, or of convincing spiritual realities in daily experience.

The unaccountable sadness and desolation that had been over me was coincident with the date of her death. There could be no reasonable doubt that my own subliminal self had received from her the tidings of her passing to the life beyond, and that while the lower consciousness did not record any definite message, it did receive the forcible impression of a great loss, a great sadness. Such an experience is not a matter of merely personal or private interest. There is nothing of more immediate concern to all humanity at the present time than the worth or worthlessness of psychic experiences.

It was not, I reflected, any more mysterious that my spirit and hers should have met as she left the mortal body than that, as a child, my spirit should have been so attracted by her: and that through all my girlhood, in the years before we ever met, she should yet have dominated my life. There was no human means of learning anything that day beyond the mere fact flashed under the sea by the cablegram. So I went alone to my room. I called on her to come. "I, too," I said, "am a spirit, though still dwelling in the physical world. Come to me; come and tell me what this means!" I implored her. In a few moments that same mysterious thrill, which I can only describe as like contact with an electric current, ran through me. I seemed to perceive that she came and stood by me, one hand resting lightly on my shoulder. I saw nothing visible; I felt nothing tangible; I heard nothing audible; and still, in some way, I seemed to actually know that she stood by me, — that her hand was on me, and that she answered in these words : " It was the only possible solution." Each word fell upon my mind distinctly, yet far apart, and as if it were a great effort to impress each one. Though there was no audible sound, yet no spoken words were ever more distinct. There seemed to me no room to doubt that this was telepathic communion, and already the truth of telepathy is as fully established by science as that of telegraphy. Telepathy is the language of the spirit ; audible speech is the language of physical organs.

The unseen world began to grow very real to me. Often, indeed, had I heard her speak of these mysteries, and her interest in psychical research was strong. " I look to see science prove Immortality," she once remarked, and the words are full of that prophetic power with which her remarkable force of insight always invested her. That science must prove immortality is the message of to-day. For there is a distinct and recognizable approach of the two worlds to each other, — the seen and the unseen. Each is flashing its signals, and the failure or the delay in a more universal recognition of these on our part is simply in not realizing that this communion must be attained through our own higher spiritual life, and not demanded or expected as mere phenomena. We have demanded that the unseen shall manifest themselves to us, — visibly, audibly, to our material senses. But while there is undoubtedly much of this phenomena, it is, at best, only begging the question. The only true, permanent, and satisfactory way to live in companionship and in communion with those who have passed through the experience of death is to live in the spirit, — to live, now and here, every day and every hour, the spiritual life. And what is this life? It is love, joy, peace. It is infinite and unfailing good-will; it is abounding love; it is meekness, and patience, and belief; it is energy in all endeavor; it is in the constant desire and effort to so live that, in the words of Phillips Brooks, "if every man lived as you do, this earth would be heaven." The problem of communion with those who have passed into the unseen lies with us rather than with them ; it lies in our own purification and exaltation of life ; for this alone offers the atmosphere — the aura — into which the higher spirits can enter.

The law of evolution is not limited to action on the physical world alone. It does not cease to operate with the attainment of physical perfection. For man is primarily a spiritual being, and only incidentally and transiently an inhabitant of the physical world. That is a mere phase, rudimental and experimental in its nature. His physical body is an instrument, by means of which, for a time, he is enabled to relate himself to the physical world. Here he does not so much live as begin to *learn how* to live.

The tragedy of life would be in its lost opportunities, were it not that a lost opportunity, when fully recognized too late for its pursuance here, is there held to await him who shall be worthy of it on the plane of life just beyond. The friendships that seem to have missed

their possible perfection here, to have failed in
what each at heart desired to realize, await
another experience to which each shall come
with finer preparation.

> " 'T is not within the force of fate
> The fate-conjoined to separate."

Whether one shall again take up his intercourse with the friend who has passed before
him into the unseen, depends on the daily life
he lives now and here. The meeting beyond
is in no sense a matter of arbitrary and mysterious destiny. It depends solely upon the
sustaining and the growth of mutual understanding between the two lives, — the one in
the seen, the other in the unseen. The future
meeting is a matter of condition, of sympathy.
It is as crude to imagine that all who die
necessarily meet, as to suppose that all Ameri-
cans who go to London or Paris inevitably
meet there and become acquainted. Whether
they do or not depends solely on the conditions that produce, or fail to produce, the
attractions that draw people together.

Man being primarily a spiritual being, his own real progress or real success in life is as he so realizes himself. The life after death is fast coming to be no longer to us a speculation or a superstition, but a very real fact with which to deal, — a phase of the near future for which to daily prepare. And the only true preparation for the life after death is to live nobly the life before death.

There seems to me no doubt that her prophetic words to the effect that science will yet prove Immortality are almost on the eve of fulfilment.

Psychic science is conquering new territory ; discerning more and more of truth constantly. It is discovering that the life just beyond this is not so great a change from this as we have fancied ; that there is no such thing as a "disembodied" spirit. Death is simply the separation of the finer ethereal body from the outer and coarser one. The new form is like the old, save that it is subtle, magnetic, and it is far more the direct reflection of the spiritual nature. The unseen

world in which it now begins another life is
as real, — far more real, indeed, — than this,
and is formed of far more potent forces.   This
world exists all about us in space.   To become cognizant of it depends on condition
alone.   To the blind the world we live in is
unseen, because the blind man has not the
organ that corresponds with his environment;
when the spiritual world about us is undis-
covered, it is because we have not yet developed those latent faculties which would enable
us to perceive it.   The spiritual life is

> "built of furtherance and pursuing :
> Not of spent deeds, but of doing."

As we live the life of the spirit, we are
companioned by the friends in the unseen, in
the simple and natural way that attends all
true relations of mutual sympathy.

PAST THE MORNING STAR.

I look to see science prove Immortality.

KATE FIELD.

" Such sweet communion had been ours
    I prayed that it might never end.
My prayer is more than answered; now,
    I have an angel for my friend."

PAST THE MORNING STAR.

" Past midnight, — past the morning star."

"IT was the only possible solution ! " These words remained with me. There was in them a significance that cannot be here translated, but I felt it and perceived its truth. Failing health and other attendant circumstances made it imperative that she should be released from the conditions here and permitted to enter new ones. Yet, a few days later, when I had searched the London papers for any added tidings and failed to find them, hope revived, and the possibility asserted itself that the cablegram had been some dreadful mistake. In a way I *knew* this was not true, and still, as a little escape from the intolerable pain, I almost sought to deceive myself into a moment's respite. I was standing before the mirror dressing for dinner, in a half-blind relief at the words of a friend who, thinking only of how to comfort me a little, had just asserted her strong belief that the news must have been a mistake and that mistakes did sometimes occur in cablegrams, — I was half in hope and half in despair trying to reinforce myself on this meagre possibility, — when again I was suddenly conscious of her presence: she stood before me and though, as before, I saw nothing visible, yet I was as conscious of her form, of the expression of her countenance, even of her dress, as I could have been of any friend who had come in. And again distinctly her words, though not audible, fell on my inner sense.

"It is true," ran the words, calling me by name; "it is true, and you must believe it." Then I knew, though I cannot explain how or why, that the reference was to her death; she had seen how I was trying, for the moment, to delude myself with a false hope, and with that passion for truth at any cost, and however unpalatable, that always pre-eminently charac-

terized her, she had been enabled to approach me nearly enough to tell me this.
The impressiveness of the presence which I
perceived, which I felt with a vividness and
a force never experienced in any meeting
here, is beyond the power of words to describe. As I went down and joined my friends
at dinner, Madame, my hostess, again ex-
claimed, " I do believe you will find that cable
to be a mistake." " No, Madame," I replied ;
" it was not a mistake ; it is true."

" But how do you know ? " she rejoined in
surprise ; " I thought you were almost convinced, since you did not find it in the London
papers, that it was not true."

How did I know, indeed ? Ah, I could not
tell her how ; yet I *did* know as well as I
do at the moment of writing this, that my
hope was an idle one, and that I must cease
all weak lament and lift my thought to
another state of existence.

The next day I again sat alone in my room
and called upon her to come. I was soon
conscious of this impressive though all unseen

presence. "Tell me," I implored, "tell me *how* we shall bridge over this gulf of silence between the Seen and the Unseen? *What* can we do, you and I, to bridge over this silence between the two planes of life? We stand here, spirit to spirit, for I, too, though still in the physical world, am potentially a spiritual being as well as you. How can you still convey to me the knowledge of your experiences?"

"It rests with you rather than with me," was the reply. No words were audible; no form was visible; but this sentence sank upon my mind with the absolute and unmistakable reality that would attend any reply made to a very serious question.

This time the words were not quite so far apart, and it seemed easier for her to speak and for me to receive them than before. "It rests with you rather than with me!" The words opened to me a new vista. The current "spiritualism" of the world has always been calling on those in the unseen life to manifest themselves; to "rap," to "materialize," — this and that. Without going into this subject at all, it may probably be received by us all as approximate truth that a proportion of all these recorded and related manifestations are true ; a proportion fraudulent, including both intentional and unintentional deception. But in any case the *onus* has been thrown upon the unseen to make themselves known to us, rather than upon ourselves to so develop our spiritual nature as to come into easy and natural communication with them.

In that other world which Kant well calls not another *place*, but another *view*, are the hosts of the unseen ; their lives press closely to ours, but are made up of a range of experiences far more extended, more vivid, more significant, than our own. How shall we comprehend these ? How shall we understand what they desire to tell us ?

It rests with us rather than with them.

Communion with this world is no more the mere experience of an hour's *séance* with a " medium " than is the mere occasional sending of a telegram the measure of our life. As potential spiritual beings, it is our privilege

to live the life of the spirit, — the higher life
of intellectual work, of affection, of generosity,
of love.   That quality of life is spiritual life.
That quality of life renders the inter-communion possible.

The evolutionary progress of the race has
now attained a degree that renders inter-
communion between the two worlds the next
step.   It is as natural, as subject to the or-
derly workings of Law, as is the development
of electricity.   This opening of inter-communion — not as an occasional phenomenon, but
as the natural daily experience — is now as
essential to the higher social progress as was
the laying of the Atlantic cable.   Is it " visionary " to talk of it?   Columbus was a visionary.
Cyrus Field was a visionary.   " Visions," says
George Eliot, " are the creators and feeders
of mankind."

The nature, the resources, the experiences
common to the life just beyond, are, we may be
assured, soon to be revealed to us.

" What is so universal as death must be a
benefit," wrote the poet Schiller; and to any

of us who have paused before the closed portal beyond which our nearest and dearest have vanished, these words must recur as significant. There is a signal comfort in realizing the universality of the experience. Even at the worst and in the most despairing view, it is only a question of time. It is not as if death occurred to some and not to others. It is the one inevitable and absolute certainty for every human being, and in this fact alone is untold consolation.

" For dying has grown dear
Now you are dead, who turned all things to grace."

Even the most despairing and sceptical pessimist must needs admit this proposition : that if immortality and reunion beyond the grave is true, it is, at worst, only a question of time. The event is assured. If immortality is not true, and if there is no reunion beyond, — if this life here is all, — then a few years more or less of happiness matter little, in the long run. The end is inevitable ; and whether it come sooner or later is not of lasting significance.

For myself, while I had always believed
entirely, though in a rather serenely light-
hearted way, in the reunion beyond, and in
more or less communion between those in the
two worlds all the time : yet when the question suddenly became to me, by *her* death,
one of the most absolute and predominant
importance, then, instead of accepting readily
the possibility of communion with her, I became questioning and critical of every experience.   In just the degree to which it was to
me a matter of supreme moment, — one that
transcended every other wish and hope and
demand of life, — to just that degree did I
grow more and more critical in scrutiny of the
experiences which I record in this story of a
summer.   It is, indeed, a story so entirely of
the inner life, and of experiences the most
sacred and private, that only the conviction
that the occurrences attest the working of a
law as yet unformulated constrains this record.   It is more and more borne in upon my
mind that, in the order of divine Providence,
the time is approaching for the beginning of

direct and authentic inter-communion between
the two worlds of the seen and the unseen.
Always have there been partial glimpses, occasional intimations, the momentary lifting of the
curtain. The poets have always had visions
of " angels that come and go," and have
transcribed them, without, perhaps, the conviction of their absolute and simple and literal reality. They have been vague, because
the mind of the one receiving them was in
the race bondage to the prevailing belief that
these things are abnormal, and are rather,
even at best, the shadow of truth than truth
itself. Theology, rather than intuition, has
dominated mankind. The Bible is one continuous record of what are really and simply
spiritual experiences, occurring between the inhabitants of the seen and the unseen worlds.
With the life of Jesus these assumed a still
higher character ; and his life, his death, his
subsequent appearances in the spiritual body,
offered an impressive object lesson of the destiny of the soul. He whose life was so far
exalted above that of any other also was ena-

bled to realize the spiritualization of his visible body, so that, instead of his spiritual form escaping from its outer sheath, as is the case in the usual process of death, his spiritual power was sufficient to transmute the physical body into the spiritual one, and thus there was no body left in the sepulchre. Psychic science has now arrived at this truth, which explains the fact that has puzzled and perplexed preceding ages, — that the sepulchre was vacant when the stone was rolled away. Psychic science advances and makes its discoveries in the same accurate and authentic manner that science on any other plane makes. That the earth is round and revolves; that the law of gravitation obtains; that action and reaction are equal; that the stars and that solar systems have their appointed courses, — all these are among the sublime truths that science has discovered. In an age that can photograph thought; that can weigh the emotions; that can send a message by a sunbeam instead of a wire; that can telegraph by the clouds, — in such an age it is not

possible that absolute ignorance shall prevail
as to the nature and the general characteristics of the life just beyond this, to which go,
every day, those nearest and dearest to us ; to
which we are inevitably destined. The time
has arrived when direct and authentic communication must begin.

"Shall I hold on with both hands to every
paltry possession?" said Emerson. "All I
have seen teaches me to trust the Creator
for all I have not seen."

Communication with those who have gone
into the unseen by means of visible forces, as
rapping, table-lifting, and all kinds of physical
phenomena, is sometimes genuine, but is, at
the best, clumsy and crude. It is calculated
to only impress the senses, and deals only with
the material. As man advances in spirituality
of life, he develops those faculties which have
a correspondence to the faculties of spiritual
beings. The difference is as it would be in
communication here, if we resorted to rapping
and table-tapping and signs and signals instead
of language. Now, if mankind could grasp the

law of telepathy and thus learn the language of spiritual life, could not the awful desolation of death, resulting from the unbroken silence, be redeemed to a sense of sacred joy?   Is not this, then, the next step in evolution ?   Is it not the achievement of the near future, — to so develop spirituality of life and the use of spiritual faculties that communion between those in this world will take on those higher instantaneous conditions of spirit to spirit, and that communion may be established between the seen and the unseen ?

The more conscious the communion with *her* became, the more I seemed to be taught that the power of telepathy is that by means of which the identity of spiritual life in both the seen and in the unseen shall be established.   It is the language of the spirit.   Undoubtedly the means of communication between those who have passed through death, and who are in the life beyond, it is no less the higher means of their communication with us here, and the higher means of communication, also, between those who are still in the physical life. It is a means possible only to a certain degree of spiritual development, united with intelligent recognition. The discovery of telepathy — the most swift, subtle, and potent force in existence — is one whose results are incalculable. For with our rational recognition these results will begin to take their due place in life and fall into the divine order of the conduct of affairs. Telepathy will inevitably become a practical working factor in life, as universally recognized as telegraphy and as definitely controlled by its own laws. When it is once understood that communication between two persons in the unseen world, or two persons in this world, or between one who is here and one who is there, is substantially the same kind of communication, then the separation of death will not separate, and the absolute and vivid perception of the divine order of the universe will begin. For the sake of clearness, let us suppose the case of four friends, all of whom are known to each other; two of whom have died and are in the unseen world, and the other two of whom are here.

A and B, we will say, are in the unseen
world; C and D are in the physical world.
Now if A and B carry on their intercourse
together by telepathy; if C and D can also,
even while in this world, communicate by
the same law; and if A and B both communicate to C and D by this swift and subtle
mental telegraphy of thought, — then it is
obvious that all four are, practically, spiritual
beings, living in a spiritual world, and in
touch with spiritual forces. It is obvious that
when C and D shall emerge, so to speak, from
their physical bodies, that they will be to some
degree prepared for the change to the new life
and the new conditions. It is also obvious
that if the spiritual nature while here can be
so developed as to be able to intelligently use
its higher faculties, — those which are its
working forces for the life to come, — it is a
valuable achievement. Every advance in
power reacts upon the environment. The
world is one thing to the savage, another to
the civilized man. The higher the civilization, the larger are the resources of life.

"The universe belongs to him who loves, who wills, who prays," says Balzac; "but he must love, he must will, he must pray." To love, to will, to pray, is to come into conscious realization of the higher powers.

There has often been quoted, with the emphasis of applause, the remark of some one who proposed to take "one world at a time." But where is the line to be drawn? Man has his twofold nature, — the physical and the spiritual. The moment that he reads, thinks, transacts business, enters into social relations, he is acting, by necessity, the part of an inhabitant of the spiritual world. Thought, love, sympathy, intelligence, — those all belong to his spiritual nature. If he is to take one world only, implying the world of the visible and the tangible, then he must merely eat, drink, and sleep. To think, to invent, to create, to conduct great enterprises, to hold social relations, — all that is of the other world, which he who consistently takes "one world at a time" must bar out from his life. The phrase is easily reduced to an absurdity.

There are very few human beings who live exclusively in the "one world." The one who did so live would be a monstrosity, for he would have to be devoid of mental power and of social sympathies.

To live the higher life is a method commended by all. What is that higher life but to live the life of the spirit, — which is joy, peace, and love? To achieve the life of the spirit is to develop within ourselves those faculties which are in easy and natural communication with the faculties of those in the unseen. It is to come into spiritual correspondence with them.

IN TWO WORLDS.

Two worlds hast thou to dwell in, Sweet, —
   The virginal, untroubled sky,
And this vext region at my feet.
   Alas, but one have I !

To all my songs there clings the shade,
   The dulling shade of mundane care;
They amid mortal mists are made,
   Thine, in immortal air.

WILLIAM WATSON.

IN TWO WORLDS.

Our eyes are holden that we cannot see things that stare us in the face until the hour arrives when the mind is ripened. Then we behold them, and the time when we saw them not is like a dream.

EMERSON.

HE law of auto-suggestion accounts for a large proportion of the experiences which those unfamiliar with the data of psychic science ascribe to the force of another mind; but it could not, it seemed to me, account for these occasional occurrences when the sudden coming of my friend in the unseen took on the same reality that would invest the arrival of any guest or caller. In fact, this is but a feeble expression to describe those vivid experiences which often reminded me of Emerson's words when he says: —

"In our definitions we grope after the spiritual by describing it as *invisible*. The true meaning of spiritual is *real*."

This was what they seemed, — *real* experiences in contrast with which the meeting and mingling with people in this life were vague. It is true that the thought of her was never, so to speak, absent from my mind. Nor did I even for an instant wish to forget, even though remembrance was pain unspeakable. Ah ! —

> " The rose's scent is bitterness
> To him that loved the rose."

And always with me, whatever the scenes of outward beauty, of historic grandeur, of poetic association, was that constant sense of desolation. Without *her* it was literally true for me that

> " the world's great space
> Held nothing but an empty place."

This perpetual consciousness of her, however, did not produce any perpetual consciousness of her presence. When that recognition came it was as distinct as that of the entrance of any visitor, besides being far more vivid and impressive. Scrutinizing these mental conditions the conviction grew that if her presence was merely a matter of imagination on my part, I should imagine it more frequently, and for longer periods of time. But it seemed to be a distinct event outside myself when I perceived her presence, and as if it were by some law as natural as that which governs our meetings in this world. It seemed, too, that she was learning how to reach me, as my spirit was endeavoring to learn how to recognize her, and that on both sides this was a spiritual experiment in which we were both gaining increased facility.

It was on the morning of the nineteenth day after she had gone to the other world that I awakened and gazed for an instant in sheer bewilderment at the space where an instant before I had seen her. The sceptic will say this was a dream; but as it links itself with so many other experiences later on that proved themselves outside those of this life, I am persuaded that the state I had been in

was merely a bodily sleep, while the spirit was
actively conscious. At all events, I seemed
to have just seen and talked with her. It
was as if we had suddenly met after a long
absence, and I was narrating to her how I
had endeavored by means of maps and data
to follow her in her last journeys when here.
She looked as I had never seen her, yet perfectly natural, if the two can be reconciled.
It was she in her radiant youth, the girl
I had never seen rather than the woman I had
known, yet the question of identity, or even
of any strangeness, did not occur to me. In
reply to my remark about following her journeys, — which applied, indeed, to the entire
fifteen years of our friendship during which
she had travelled extensively and I had been
so in touch with her plans that almost any
day, if not hour, I could have reached her
by telegram, — in reply she said, with an in-
effable smile, "Ah, but there was *one* journey
on which you could not follow me." It was
at this moment that I came to consciousness ;
and should any caller in my room suddenly

vanish from the chair in which he sat, I could not be more amazed than I was for an instant to see the vacant place where I had just seen her.

Is it not true that the "subconscious" self is an infelicitous name for the higher, the real self, whose powers are far in advance of those manifested on this or the visible plane? This subconscious (or higher) self is to the ordinary self as the man who can hear, see, speak, touch, and walk is to the one who is deaf, blind, dumb, and paralyzed. Clairvoyance, clairaudience, the power to control things far beyond our actual touch and presence, are potential faculties of every human being. Jesus plainly said that all He had done we should do; and not only this, but "greater things." The key to all true life is to accept His assertions in the simple, direct way in which they are given. The potential higher being, with all its marvellous powers, is within each human being. To realize this divinity in every-day living is the desired end. By virtue of this potential higher self we have commu-

nion with those beyond death. To just the
extent that we realize on this plane of manifestation that higher spiritual (or subconscious) self, to that extent do we dwell, now
and here, in the spiritual world, in communion with its inhabitants.

It was, I am persuaded, my own " subconscious," or subliminal self which, from some
cause of unusual harmony at that time, was
able to distinctly perceive and recognize the
ethereal form of my friend. The first three impressions of her presence had been of messages
heard by the inner sense. In this fourth one
was the inner sense of sight added to hearing.
The sensation it left with me is indescribable
in its exhilaration and radiant energy.

It is now nearly fifty years since the sound of
" the Rochester knockings " was heard round
the world. From that time a vast mass of
phenomena has accumulated that has been
studied, denied, derided, accepted, variously.
It has enlisted learned investigation. It has
baffled investigation. It has been relegated
to the realm of the inconsequential, and has

incited the frequent remark that it is all too crude and too idle to have any high origin or convey any hint of value. This sweeping generalization would be not without truth if all this were an end. But it was not in the least an end, but a means. It was simply the method employed to arrest the general attention. The finer and higher method of telepathy might reach and impress the brain of an Emerson, but it could not reach and impress the general public. That had to be done by the appeal to the physical senses, — to the sight, the hearing, and the touch. To communicate by rapping and the alphabet may seem very puerile, but what beginning could be made? How was this gulf of silence between the two worlds to be bridged over? What signals could be flashed across? All that stage has been merely preparatory. The real illumination is yet to come.

But the achievement is to be on our side, by lifting ourselves to the spiritual life; by so overcoming the lower, the selfish nature that we may perpetually live the life of the spirit. The devotee who embraces the ascetic life seizes a fragment of the truth, — that of overcoming the lower physical nature. But physical qualities held in due support of the powers of the spirit are not low. For instance, to dine for the mere pleasure of appetite is a propensity to be overcome; but to dine for the reinforcement of bodily energies, that they may well sustain that instrument through which the spirit works, is a factor in the higher life. It is a life that is lived by considering the body as an instrument, — as the temple of the indwelling spirit, — to be kept in health and in harmony, in support of the spiritual purposes of accomplishment, of aspiration, of the fulfilment of duties, the radiation of noble and true influence. So living, spirit will respond to spirit, both from the Seen and the Unseen.

Nor, when this matter is looked at fairly, can it seem irreverent or idle to endeavor to trace the law of social relation which persists beyond death. Just why it should be wrong or unwise to establish, if possible, clearly recognized and intelligent communion with those who have passed into the higher state is not quite plain. Might it not, with equal force, have been said, before the Atlantic cable was laid, that it would be wrong to attempt instantaneous communication between the two continents, — on the ground that it was unnatural? If it is right to continue communication with a friend on the other side of the earth, how can it be wrong to continue communication with him on the other side of death?

We are in the dawning of an age of higher forces. The more active, the more potent, the more vivid world is as the plane just beyond this. There is the sphere of far wider and more important activities, and it is of these that we catch certain reflections and suggestions, as in the great inventions here which are projected from that plane to this. There is the centre of intense and far-reaching activities; there is, indeed, the real life, in the sense of deeper realities than those of the present stage. Now, the capacity to receive impressions is of itself a valuable quality. As humanity advances, this capacity becomes more keen, and man catches hints and receives intimations of a finer and far more extended order. The result of these is seen in the world at the present time, in the growing knowledge of science, the increasing inventions, the general advance to a larger scale of living. This advance will increase in an accelerated ratio, until this world shall be fairly transformed to a higher plane. But the transformation will not be a supernatural, but a purely natural one. Some of these transformations have already been entered upon. It is difficult to imagine the social state when there was no telegraphic communication, no steam-engine, no fast steamers. Yet within the memory of men still living was the time when it required a month to go to Europe; when only the stagecoach went to the Pacific Coast, and when telegraphic communication did not exist. Even electricity, which is undoubtedly the force in use on the plane of life beyond this, is so extending the facilities of life on earth as to, practically, enlarge all the faculties of the mind and increase the use of the senses. If by telephone one may speak to a friend one thousand miles away, that is practically working the miracle of his voice being heard at the distance of one thousand miles.

Space is being annihilated by steam and by electricity. The isolation of life is also being rapidly transformed into close social contact by the new conditions.

The curiously misleading phraseology of death as "going into the dark," and as "the terror of the unknown," and "the land of shadows" will soon be obsolete. Humanity will recognize the higher truth.

DISTANT GATES OF EDEN.

" The connection between electricity and psychic force is a subject of singular interest; and the tendency of facts already known goes far to prove that they are connected. . . .

" Each force in nature is the servant of the next above it. Mechanics lends itself to chemistry; chemistry to electricity; electricity to psychic force. And these are but the outer gates to the vital forces entrusted to a higher range of spiritual existence."

" Who, rowing hard against the stream,
    Saw distant gates of Eden gleam."

In our definitions we grope after the spiritual by describing it as *invisible*. The true meaning of spiritual is *real*. — EMERSON.

OMMUNICATION is the supreme test of civilization. The higher its degree, the finer its quality, the more easy and swift are the methods of communication. Take the savage, the barbarous state ; how abject and dull are the methods of social intercourse ! Conversation, in the sense of the higher development of life, is unknown. Whatever intercourse there is, is restricted to the crudest and most meagre kind, and relates only to the barest physical necessities. As the scale of life ascends, the range of communication increases, and its subjects multiply. The man of the higher culture has a thousand subjects on which to converse, a multitude of ideas to impart, that are totally unknown to a lower degree of development. Then, as we advance in the scrutiny of civilized life, we see the small town with its one weekly paper, the larger one with its daily, the great city with its dozens of semi-daily papers, — all eagerly seized as methods of intercommunication in human society. As civilization advances, the barriers of all isolation break down. Each nation is aware of the leading events transpiring in other nations; conversation, letters, the daily press, the telegraph, the cable, the telephone, — all these are the expressions of the highest development of civilization. Easy and rapid transit also keeps pace with these. So much must be conceded as an existing and evident truth.

Now, the next step in the higher development of life is to establish communication with the life just beyond this. If there is any advantage in direct and swift communication with other nations, how much greater may be that of direct and intelligent communication with the higher plane of life! If it is desir-

able to establish communication with the inhabitants of Mars, how much more so with
that vast multitude of our own friends, our
own fellow-beings, who have, by means of the
process of death, attained a state of existence
that is still a mystery to us, as regards its conditions, its methods, its resources. Here is a
vast world of the most vivid and important
activities, — a world whose life is infinitely
more active, more significant than that of our
own, — and we go on for centuries regarding
it as a misfortune to go there, and as a place
which we call the land of shadows, of darkness, of phantoms! More important than the
mission of Columbus to discover this new
continent; more important than the mission
of Cyrus Field to lay the cable, — is the mission to establish a direct, an intelligent, and
an authoritative communication with those in
the next plane of life.

The telegraph, the telephone, thought transference, — here we have the ascending scale
of communication : the telegraph for the brief-
est messages of utility, the telephone for still

more expanded and easy conversational intercourse, thought transference, or psychic
telegraphy, for the still more swift, more individual, more extended and satisfying inter-
change. It is in this that the possibilities lie
of direct communication with those who have
passed beyond death. The cruder forms of
physical phenomena served their purpose to
arrest the attention of a cruder age. It is for
this age to develop the method of psychic
communion. It would seem, indeed, that
humanity is already on the threshold of new
and finer phases of psychical experience and
convincing evidence of the close relations existing between the Seen and the Unseen
worlds. If science has not yet proved Immortality, it has certainly penetrated very near to
some of the conditions of the life just beyond
this. Many of these conditions are adapted
to the higher development of this life. For
instance, the X ray of Roentgen enables the
physical eye to penetrate a solid substance, as
before its discovery the speculative thinker
believed only the spiritual eye could do. By

means of the telephone, man becomes practically clairaudient. The invention whereby one may be enabled to see as well as to hear, at the distance of a thousand miles, is on its way to being perfected. Now, the annihilation of space is, distinctively, a condition which has always been associated with man's ideas of the spiritual world, where to think, or to will, was to be. But through marvellous, although natural inventions, the inhabitants of this world are coming to enter somewhat upon these conditions. The arrangements being made for the test and trial and exhibition of electrical apparatus at the Exposition of 1900 in Paris almost surpass imagination. To be propelled through the air, as it were, on wires from the Eiffel Tower to the dome of the Trocadero, by the electric motor, is almost equal to flying through the air. The photography of thought, which is an accomplished fact ; the marvellous preservation of the voice in the phonograph, — these and other of the new discoveries of hitherto latent forces of nature are impressive indications of the manner in which the spiritual insight and energy of man are penetrating the secrets of the universe.

It is, perhaps, not illogical to reason that the life just beyond death is one that differs from ours only in that of this higher and larger knowledge of controlling the laws of nature.

Dr. Edward O. Day in a recent article says : —

" The Sanscrit logicians declare that, apart from the physical or gross body, which disintegrates at death, there exists an ethereal or ' subtile body,' which, though material, is so subtile as thus far to have escaped the investigations of science; that this, not the gross body, is the perceiver, actor, and director of the personality ; that it uses the physical body as an instrument, but at the same time receives impressions from it in varying degrees of intensity proportioned to their higher or lower rates of vibration, — coarser or finer materiality. These impressions are said to impart an indelible coloring to the ' subtile body.'

"At death this 'subtile body' is said to go out with a definite rate of vibration, — which predetermines the succeeding stage of experience. Saint Paul may refer to this when he says: 'There is a natural body and a spiritual body;' and when he questions 'With what body do they come?' is it not this spiritual body to which reference is made?"

Almost the only practical difference to-day between the conservative and the more advanced views of spiritual belief is that while both believe in the immortality of the soul, the one regards death as final separation from those remaining on this plane of life. If A is to outlive B for fifty years, then must he wait fifty years before again having companionship with his friend; while the newer belief is that between B in the Unseen and A in the Seen there may be a perpetual intercourse of spirit to spirit. Thus, if A felt himself constantly companioned, it would not only infinitely lessen all the anguish of bereavement, but would be the constant stimulus to live that higher life of the spirit; that life

which is joy, peace, and love, — that life
whose joy, peace, and love can only be
wrought out of the moral virtues of truth,
honesty, courtesy, and flawless integrity. In
fact, this belief gives the most remarkable
impetus to the spiritualization of life.

Not, of course, that one desires to believe
what is not true. Who would consent to
dwell in a fool's paradise? If death is the entire separation from those dearest to us until
we, too, die, then by all means let us know it,
let us recognize and accept it. Even that belief is not without its consolations, for death is
the one certain and inevitable experience that
awaits us all. It would be, at most, only a
question of time.

Still it is, indeed, less as a matter of personal consolation and comfort — great as is
the factor of personal happiness in life — than
it is as a matter of the higher development;
of responsive interest in being in touch with
the life of the higher plane, that the realization of immediate intercourse between the
two worlds is of greatest value. The mere

phenomenon — which is only associated with the presence of a medium — is merely the rudimentary stage of this finer realization. Its principal service has been to establish the reality of the close relation between the two planes of life. It is at best a clumsy mechanism; but it is a question whether any other means than that appealing to the physical senses would ever have succeeded in arousing popular interest. For half a century these physical manifestations have been on trial, as it were, and that they are now generally accepted as having in them elements impossible to explain on any other hypothesis is conceded.

The general recognition and acceptance of the truth that the life beyond this is more real, even as mature life is more real than childhood, is so rapidly increasing that it amounts to a new development in the human race. More important even than this is the recognition that the spiritual world is a matter of condition; that it can be experienced before death; and that just in proportion as life is elevated and noble and generous and loving, in that proportion does one live in the spiritual or the more real world. "Thoughts let us into realities," said Emerson. To just that degree in which one lives in the spirit may there be communication or communion between the two worlds. The religious term has always been "communion," signifying the meeting and mingling of mind. The term "communication" has come to be regarded as phenomenon, which again is widely discussed and criticised as being genuine or fraudulent. But any communion at all is certainly communication, although it may be in the higher region of impressions rather than the one of definite messages. That form is, too, more desirable, even though there may be at times legitimate desire for special word or message regarding some specific matter. But the church has always recognized the possibility and the actual existence of communion, and has held the "communion of the saints" to be among the richest spiritual blessings.

Edgar Fawcett has recently said : —

" From Sir Francis Galton, an English astron-
omer of wide repute, comes the tidings that
Mars is sending us signals, and that he has
already resolved these into sentences, and the
sentences he has separated into letters.   It is a
celestial cipher, affirms Sir Francis Galton, but
one of which he has not yet found the key.
Some huge electric invention has been constructed by the Martians, and planetary currents are made so subservient to its enormous
energies that an incessant telegraphy is going
on with interstellar ether for its medium.
Working in one of the great European obser-
vatories, Sir Francis has constructed, it is de-
clared, an apparatus which he placed next to
the telescope he employed, and which has
given him the most amazing results.   He is
now convinced that earnest efforts are being
made by Mars to hold with us intelligent converse.   ' He has not yet been able to decipher
the exact meaning of these words which the
Martian telegraph operators have been flashing
toward us,' runs a startling article full of
apparent veracity, ' but that they constitute
long messages, and are meant to be read by
the inhabitants of the earth, he has no doubt.'

"Now suppose that all this budget of seeming miracle has fact for its base. Interplanetary communication is not really more wonderful than intercontinental communication — than the leagues of cable which already wed Europe to the west. And yet if the people on Mars should ever speak with us, how transcendently mighty would be the epoch! Every event in history would pale before it."

When a scholarly writer who is in no wise inclined toward spiritual speculation yet declares that " Interplanetary communication is not really more wonderful than intercontinental communication," it registers the amazing advance of the thought of the day.

The interplanetary communication seems a possible and a reasonable thing. Not less so, but more, seems the probable, the inevitable establishment of communication, in recognized, definite form, between the visible and the ethereal worlds, or between those here and those who have passed beyond death. In the sense of communion the process is telepathy. There is probably far more of that going on with each and all than any one is fully aware, for just what thoughts may be suggested by the invisible companions, and just what the mind itself suggests in its action is by no means discriminated. Yet with attention and with sufficient growth of spiritual life, this form of communication — the highest and most satisfactory — may grow clear and recognizable. One may come to realize the thought, or the words, of the invisible companion as definitely as those of any caller or visitor or companion in this life.

This recognition grew to me constantly more clear and definite in relation to her. About this time I left Paris for a long journey through southern Europe. From the hour of entering Switzerland until we reached Vienna, the route through the Alps and the Tyrol was one of picturesque and poetic beauty. Never could we forget the atmospheric effects through the Tyrol, where clouds and peaks combined in mythological forms till one fairly saw the gods of Hellas towering in the sky. While in Vienna, once in the marvellous cathedral of

6

Saint Stephen, and again on an enchanted afternoon with Madame Materna, while with her in the rose-garden that glows and gleams in the grounds of her beautiful villa, there were recognitions on my part of a presence invisible to others, but not in a way sufficiently striking to relate. Later came a visit to Hungary, where every hour was full of activities; a journey to Venice *via* Fiume, around the blue Adriatic, and then — Venice. Her towers and marble palaces rose from the water like a dream, like a mirage, like a magician's spell; and one felt the thrill of the vague memory, —

> " Of a life lived somewhere, I know not
> In what diviner sphere — "

And in the strange silence of this dream city I again began to realize *her* companionship.

Experiences grew still more vivid during an evening journey, after Venice had faded like a wraith in the distance, and the route lay through a region where the purple peaks of the Apennines were swimming in a sea of silver mist. They deepened and multiplied while in Florence, where more than once invisible guidance led me to place or picture that otherwise I should have missed.

At the same time general assertions of this nature carry no weight, and this little record must limit itself to such experiences as can be more definitely stated.

UNTO MY HEART THOU LIVEST SO.

For you cannot talk of matter alone. If you say matter, you must say spirit. They are the two sides of the one existence, and are never to be separated from each other in fact, although in thought we distinguish them by quality, in order that we may be able to think at all. But in manifestation they are never apart. There is no such thing as spirit, or force, or life, without matter, by which it takes its form, by which it shows its energy.

ANNIE BESANT.

"How can I cease to pray for thee? Somewhere
    In God's great universe thou art to-day.
Can He not reach thee with His tender care?
    Can He not hear me when for thee I pray?

"What matters it to Him who holds within
    The hollow of His hand all worlds, all space,
That thou art done with earthly pain and sin?
    Somewhere within His ken thou hast a place.

"Somewhere thou livest and hast need of Him;
    Somewhere thy soul sees higher heights to climb;
And somewhere still there may be valleys dim
    That thou must pass to reach the hills sublime."

" Sometimes wherever I may go
  Unto my heart thou livest so,
  I marvel if the forms I meet,
  The speech I hear, be Time's deceit, —
  If viewlessness and silence screen
  More life than can be heard and seen."

O far from the relations between friends being ended by death, it is only then that they begin. Then, if they are real, a readjustment takes place that perfects the mutual sympathy and comprehension. If there is no true spiritual relation but only the so-called friendship of the convenience of the moment, or of external attraction, the event of death terminates it, even as it deepens and enlarges all real relations.

" The rose that blossomed not
    Lives in our hearts forever,
  And hands ne'er clasped in life
    Death has no power to sever."

A very potent and marvellous uplifting to
the diviner world is the invariable experience
after one most beloved has gone on into the
invisible realm. The readjustment of relations
begins to take place. It is life that separates;
it is death that unites. While the spirit is inhabiting the physical body it is screened, im-
prisoned, as it were; and the assertion of a
German philosopher, that no man ever saw or
ever was seen by his fellow-man, is literally
true.

> " You do not see my friend at all ;
> You see what hides him from your sight,"

well writes a poet. "Spiritual things are
spiritually discerned;" and to recognize each
other truly, even while here, we must all be
discerners of spirits. Life is just as sacred as
death. We are building up our spiritual relationships and conditions every hour and
every day; and to just the degree in which one
can live in the spirit here, and regard all his
friendships as spiritual relationships, — so to
that extent does he transcend death, and es-

tablish, here and now, the conditions that this change cannot destroy nor greatly affect.

When the spiritual being that has lived a certain period here slips out of its physical body and is free from material clogs and limitations, the readjustment in a number of ways is made. Those who still remain in this world are far more truly recognized. Some have been unduly appreciated; some have been underestimated. The risen spiritual being, now being able to discern spiritual states and to adjust all to a new scale of values, rearranges his loves and friendships, so to speak. In fact, here is the type of the judgment day.

Instead of any sadness or despair when death comes near to us, the true view is simply one of exaltation and of happiness, heretofore undreamed.

The evidence of immortality, and of sweet, swift communion between the visible and the invisible worlds, is in one's own soul.

"The witness is within," as Whittier truly says. To talk of so-called "spiritualism" and "mediums" as the final tests or as the arbiters of a future life, in which to believe or not to believe, according as to whether a " communication " seems genuine or not, is a moral state so puerile and so insignificant as to be unworthy extended allusion, — much less discussion. It is nothing less than sacrilege to hear a man say that he rests his faith or unfaith, — his belief or his disbelief in Immortality and the divine life, the life more abundant that is entered by the process we call death, — that he bases this faith on the fact of a " medium's " giving or not giving him a message from his relative or his friend who has died. If he have no realization of his own spiritual nature; if he does not perceive and feel and recognize the realities of the higher life in which it is his privilege to live even while in the physical body, — then no "tests" are of the slightest importance. But, once realizing himself as a spirit here and now, and recognizing his true relations to the spiritual world, then he may, under certain conditions, find the same added joy in exchanging messages with his friend in the other life that he would find in correspondence, or in visits in this life. It is simply the extension of friendly intercourse.

The conditions for this extension of intercourse between the Seen and the Unseen are to live in the spirit here and now. " The committal of the soul to God," as Professor Amiel well phrases it, is the one condition of the perception of spiritual life. You " belong to God." And " if one belongs to God, he must live worthily of Him." He " keeps an open mind to divine instruction." The communion with the Unseen is continually possible, and to some degree is continually carried on.

Still, while phenomena are less important than the unerring perception of intuition and spiritual recognition, it would be ignorance or falsehood to deny that there is definite and authentic communication between one in this world and one in the world beyond made possible by the peculiar organization of certain persons termed mediums, or psychics. One of these had prophesied to me, a number of years ago, that I should go to Europe with the

friend referred to in these pages. Two years
later the same prophecy from the same psychic
was repeated. At that time it had grown
more improbable than even at first, and, re-
marking on this to the medium, the reply was,
" It will be ; I see you there together."

It was on the June Sunday that I sat by
the grave of Mrs. Browning in the English
Cemetery at Florence that this prophecy
flashed upon my remembrance. That *she* went
to the higher life the very day of my landing
at Liverpool ; that all the story here narrated
had been lived ; that I had been so curiously conscious of her presence and companionship in a way that had increased constantly,
— were facts that, to the most incredulous
mind, could not but have been startling.

On returning from Europe, I communicated
this prophecy, and the curious coincidence of
date, at least, if not (as I believed) the fulfilment of it, to Dr. Richard Hodgson, the
eminent and critical scholar and thinker who
is the Secretary of the Society for Psychical
Research. Dr. Hodgson was impressed by

it, and promised that I should again have a
" sitting " with the psychic, whom I had not
seen for a number of years and who, in the
mean time, had come to be under the auspices
of the Society and could only be seen by offi-
cial permission. Professor James of Harvard
University, Professor Sidgwick of Cambridge,
England, Mr. F. W. H. Myers, and other
learned men had studied and tested this
psychic, and the result was a conviction that
the phenomena which occurred through her
were inexplicable on any other theory than
that of communication from those in the life
just beyond. By Dr. Hodgson's courtesy I
went to this lady for a sitting, which has
subsequently been followed by several others.
On the first occasion there were written
(through the automatic writing of the psychic) some two hundred pages signed with
the name of the friend referred to in this book.
But the signature was as unimportant a fea-
ture in the communication itself as is the signature of any personal letter from a familiar
friend. Not only various characteristic forms

of expression, strong individualities, and allusions, and circumstances were evident; but besides a clear and rational explanation of a matter that had been perplexing was given, — an explanation involving the story of an event of which I, at that time, had never heard, with its place, time, and participants all written out, and which afterward, I learned from one of the persons involved, to have been entirely correct. Still, however remarkable was the nature of this first interview, it is hardly to be compared to subsequent ones. In fact, the narration of all these up to the present time would offer a story to test the credulity of any one ; and still — and it is this fact which is the key-note of the book, which is my *raison d'être* for writing it at all, — still, this entire story of the several long communications received through this psychic, is one that is, by its very nature, provable before any tribunal. Let any jury of fair and intelligent men — with no predilections in favor of the possibility of its truth, but who were simply intelligent and just — let any such jury

be called, and the communications themselves
be submitted, and the living witnesses called
who could, and would, corroborate assertions,
allusions, and circumstances, and the verdict
of authenticity and genuineness would be
inevitable.

In no wise am I a special pleader for the
thing called Spiritualism. In common with
all sincere persons my only desire is to perceive
and to believe the truth.

To relate here the story of this train of evi-
dences would require an octavo volume; and
also, as will readily be recognized, such a narra-
tive would be of too personal a nature to quite
admit of public record. Still, while personal,
it is not, necessarily, private. The life and
deeds of a woman simple, noble, truthful, sincere, great in heart and in mind, does not
involve secrets, so to speak. One may have
scruples of delicacy against relating matters
which are, after all, open enough to every one
interested.

On one occasion I had asked her the
question, "Can you read writing — ordinary

manuscript?" The reply was: "Of course I can, but I can read your soul better. I see your thoughts most clearly." Again the question was asked, "Can you — the spiritual beings in the spiritual world — read our books, — the general literature here?" To which was replied, "No, dear, not exactly, yet the idea is understood by us." "Can you hear me if I read aloud to you?" "Yes, perfectly. Speaking aloud has an effect. It reaches us better and clearer." "Is the other life as different from ours here as we have thought?" "Oh, no, dear; it is just like going from one room into another. It is so beautiful, and there is such freedom and clearness of thought. I never struggle with my own mind here. And the travelling is delightful. The sensation of riding through the air is delicious." "Is the communication between you and myself more direct than is usual between two who are on the different planes, — the Seen and the Unseen?" "Yes, it may be said to be, because there are few persons who are so near each other." At one sitting the spirit friend took the initiative and wrote : " Dearest ——, come near to me and answer a few questions." The questions were asked, — regarding the disposition of certain affairs, and other matters, — showing as clear memory and perception of events and circumstances as would have been shown had the friends met in this world after a separation.

Naturally, the personal matters which taste forbids me to narrate would be evidential in their nature, while questions and responses of this impersonal kind are not. This is a difficulty which forms an inexorable limitation in any writing upon this subject.

The teachings of religion, while holding in essence the deepest truth, have been so largely figurative that they have left the ideas of the life beyond in a maze of abstract mystery. There is a mystic beauty in the picture of standing before the throne of God holding palm branches, but it is one that must be received in its mystic sense and not translated literally. Truth and fact are by no means synonymous. The one is eternal, the other transient.

7

It is the province of psychic science to pro-
ject its discoveries of the nature of the life
beyond this.   Religion, in its usual teachings,
gives the great truths in mystical and figurative
phrase.   To recognize the Divine Father and
Jesus the Christ, and to know that He is the
way, the truth, and the life ; to accept the
truth of the immortal nature of the soul, — this
is the supremely important matter; but as
intelligent beings, who, by the law of evolution, are developing into constantly higher
states, it may be as much a part of the true
province of knowledge to extend the domain
of investigation into the forces of spirit, as
well as into those of nature.   It is no less
reverent, surely, to inquire into the nature
and destiny of the soul than it is to inquire
into the nature and use of any form of the divine creation.   The intelligent and faithful
student of psychic science is working toward
the discovery of the new immaterial world, as
Columbus was toward the discovery of a new
continent.   In fact, as the two hemispheres of
the East and the West correspond, so are this

world and that just beyond death in correspondence. The infinite progression of the
soul is in states or series of lives. The one
lying just beyond this does not differ from
ours so greatly as has been believed. It is
not a vague region somewhere in inconceivable space, where inconceivable beings wave
palm branches ; but a world differing from
this only in degree, and by a difference hardly
more marked than that which lies between the
New England of 1620 and of 1900. If one
should dwell for a moment upon this land
as the Pilgrims found it, and on the meagre
resources up to 1800 and later, as compared
with the resources and activities of the past
half-century, and more especially of those of
the present decade, he will realize how the
constantly growing control of higher forces of
nature transforms the life of man. Take away
the steam-engine, the telegraph, the electric
motor, the submarine cable, the telephone, to
say nothing of the many other still more marvellous inventions and projections of modern
science, — and how barren and meagre and

limited is the life of man! Without the
steam-engine the distance from Boston to
New York becomes a matter of six or seven
days, rather than hours, making the two cities,
practically, as far apart as New York and
London. Without the telegraph and cable,
life in every city or town is local and insu-
lated from all the rest of the world.

Now, take that still higher control of
forces which is found in the ethereal world,
and what is the result? Our friends who
have been liberated into that larger life by the
process we name death find themselves in a
realm where will and thought are forces. To
will is to accomplish. The ethereal body is
no longer subject to the law of gravitation.
It is under the law of attraction. Communication is carried on by that subtle and swift
spiritual process of thought transference, or
telepathy, which is the spirit language, and of
which those in this world are already gaining
some knowledge. Travelling is accomplished
by floating at will through the air, — a sensation said to be a delicious one. In this ethe-

real world a life similar to this, only higher and finer in degree, is lived. There are libraries, temples of worship, halls of music, and art. There are the occupations of reading, writing, study, invention. The law of service prevails in a diviner way than here, but one that, after all, would be quite possible here; for this life may be divinely lived. The doctrine of the Incarnation is the great lesson in divine living, here and now. " God is the only reality ; and we are real only so far as we are in His order and He in us." Truly, indeed, as faith varies, so does the life that comes of it.

ACROSS THE WORLD I SPEAK
TO THEE.

" Spirits are not finely touched,
But to fine issues."

" From wave and star and flower
Some effluence rare
Was lent thee, — a divine but transient dower.
Thou yield'st it back from eyes and lips and hair
To wave and star and flower."

ACROSS THE WORLD I SPEAK TO THEE.

"Across the world I speak to thee;
  Whether in yonder star thou be
  A spirit loosed in purple air;
  Whether beneath the tropic-tree
  The cooling night-wind fans thy hair, —
  Whether in yonder star thou be,
  Across the world I speak to thee.
  Send thou a messenger to me."

THERE is coming to be a great change in the mental attitude toward death. Every sympathetic observer of life must recognize the increasing spirituality of the general feeling in regard to that event which sooner or later comes into every home, — death. Its darkness and extreme terror have almost disappeared; the time has gone when we affirmed by our lips, but denied by our conduct, our belief in immortality. Formerly — and much of it lingers at the present time — a death

in the family plunged every member of it
" into mourning." Usually the mourning is
synonymous with grief, but not invariably.
Whether it is the accompaniment of grief or
only the conventional tribute to custom, it
is a matter involving the element of trade
and traffic; of the intrusion of bustle and
material affairs on hours that should be sacred
to exaltation and to consecrated thought.
Here is a great, new experience. One dearly
beloved has gone on to the next higher plane
of life. He is not dead; he is more alive than
ever before; near and dear as the relations to
him may have been on earth, now they may
be infinitely nearer and dearer. Lowell expresses this truth in these lines : —

> " Now I can love thee truly,
>   For nothing comes between
> The senses and the spirit,
>   The seen and the unseen."

Nor need death be thought of as formless
and vague and void. " There is a natural
body and there is a spiritual body," said Saint
Paul. Psychic science has discovered and

formulated, beyond question of doubt, certain truths about the life that lies just beyond this. These truths are as unquestionably attested as any truths of philosophy or of physics.

First, " a spirit " is simply the spiritual being in the spiritual body, just as the individual here is the spiritual being in the physical body. The spiritual and the physical bodies correspond in all details of form. But the spiritual body is light and capable of swift movement, and is far more the expression of the spirit force than is the physical body. The physical body is subject to the resistance of matter, while the spiritual body is not; the one is subject to the law of gravitation, not so the other. The man living in the present life is essentially a spirit; he does not " become " one by death, but merely slips out of the outer, coarser, physical body, and finds himself in this spiritual body with head and hands and feet, — the form he has been accustomed to. Now he has to do with finer agencies. Not necessarily is he remote from the space where those on earth are living.

He has achieved a higher plane of consciousness than he had here ; but that does not
necessarily imply a geographical or astronomi-
cal change of place.   This truth is readily
recognized by a moment's reflection on the
way numerous and varied grades of life may
go on within the same physical space, from
the "insensate clod" to the insect, the animal, the human being; from the criminal to
the saint.

The event of death does not probably at
once change a man's nature.   It effects no
miraculous or instantaneous change in the
quality of his spirit.   There are spirits still in
the physical body much more exalted than
some who have gone out of the physical body.
Still, the general tendency is upward, for the
one fact of the loss of relations with material
things tends to spiritualization.

It is more than probable that there is never
a time when the friend here can be so much
aid and comfort to the one he holds dear as
just after that one has passed through death.
" You can do nothing more for him," is some-

times heard. " His life is closed." " He has gone forever." Never were words more misleading. His friend can do more than ever for him. His life is *not* closed, but — begun. He has *not* "gone forever," but rather he is nearer, closer, in more tender relation than was heretofore permitted him to be. The masses for the dead in the Catholic Church rest on the deepest spiritual truth. And how beautiful are the sacred words of which the first lines are, —

" Eternal rest give unto them, O Lord, and let perpetual light shine upon them."

To hold sacred and peaceful the season of death is to enter into its most divine uplifting. Violent grief must be torture to the one who is gone, and who is vainly striving to make those here understand that he is only more alive than they are, — alive with a keener, finer, more exalted life. The truly enlightened vision will yet come to regard death as a sacred festival, a spiritual sacrament, instead of a time of tears and seclusion and sel-

fish grief, — for, however unconsciously, such
grief *is* selfish; instead of this, it will be a
period when the nearer friends will lift up
their hearts with a new and deeper sense of
the spiritual life; when spirit to spirit — the
one in the life beyond, the other in this life —
shall meet more nearly, more truly responsive
than ever before, and a closer sense of the
divine love encompass them round about.

"The unknown is not by any necessity the
unknowable," said Bishop Phillips Brooks. In
that assertion there lies a profound truth, to
which one of almost equal significance might be
added; namely, that the effort to investigate
the unknown, and if possible to transmute it
into the known, is not demoralizing. On the
contrary, the entire progress of the world has
depended on those persons who did not regard ignorance as synonymous with righteous-
ness; whose horizon of possibilities was not
bounded by the perceptions of the senses;
who did not fear to take risks and steer into
the unknown. That the Copernican theory
of the universe replaced the Ptolemaic is due

to the faith of Galileo in new and independent investigation. The discovery and establishment of the law of gravitation is due to Newton's higher penetration into nature's laws. The constant progress of electrical science, which is revolutionizing all the conditions of modern life, is due to faith, insight, experiment ; to patient and persistent endeavor ; to unwearied effort in the pursuit of new forces. The law of psychical communication will be discovered by the same power of patient, persistent effort ; by critical scrutiny of all alleged messages received and close study of the conditions involved. Faith is not credulity ; nor is denial, and refusal to study and consider, any mark of a superior intelligence.

> " The spirit world around this world of sense
> Floats like an atmosphere."

All life that is spiritual life, whether in the physical or the psychical body, — that is, whether before death or after death, — is of this atmosphere. The spiritual world is a condition and not a location. It will readily be seen from analogies in this world how very different degrees of life can go on in the same space. Take any one block of a city, even any two homes next door to each other, or even any two rooms in one house, and consider how, under the same roof, in what is practically the same material space, two individual lives may go on, — the one exalted, noble, open to every divine influence; the other, poor, mean, dwarfed, darkened. Thus it will be seen that in the same space the spiritual and physical worlds may coexist, each being a condition.

There is a supreme need in the life of to-day : that theology shall lift itself to spirituality. Religion is not an argument, or even a creed : it is life and love ; it is the recognition of spiritual laws. "To make habitually a new estimate, that is elevation." Religion needs to take account of the new estimate, of that vast and momentous array of psychic truth that is the discovery of this age. The treasure-stores of the invisible realm are open to the spiritual perception of the present. Telepathy is not merely the phenomenal means of communication between two persons who are widely separated by distance; but it is also the appointed means by which the inhabitants of the invisible world are giving us of their knowledge, their counsel. To be able to receive this one must live in touch with the higher life, — that is, he must himself live the higher life of love, sweetness, sympathy. He must live "as seeing Him who is invisible." Falsehood, hatred, wrong-doing of any kind build up a barrier between those in this life and in the one beyond. In so far as there are moral defects, there is not spiritual life. To hold communion with friends in the life beyond, one must lift himself to that life. He must spiritualize his conditions of thought, of aspiration.

There is perhaps no power that organized religion could bring to bear on general life which would be so all-compelling in its results as to impress the reality of communion between the visible and the invisible. In the light of that realization every noble aspiration is intensified; every ignoble one revealed in

8

its true paltriness and meanness. The life that is possible in its resplendence, its exaltation, its loveliness, its charm, is seen in vivid contrast with a mere existence of worry, care, perplexity, and strife. It is not so much that if one lives nobly he shall go to beautiful conditions at death; it is that he shall have the beautiful conditions: the realization of intercourse with the invisible world here and now. Here, not merely hereafter: now, not in some vague and far off eternity.

In the natural evolution of progress the time is now approaching for a new revelation of the life just beyond the event we call death. Nearly nineteen hundred years ago Jesus, the Christ, gave the revelation suited to the comprehension of that time, and which has sufficed for the growing advancement of the centuries since. The law of progress that prevails in the divine creation has now brought the human race to that point where it is prepared to comprehend more completely the conditions and experiences beyond. This need will be met. We stand on the threshold of a new revelation.

As Bishop Brooks with his illuminated spiritual vision so clearly foresaw, the special will and purpose of God and the corresponding activity of man must produce a mutualness of knowledge. Jesus "knew the Father by a direct perception of kindred life." Herein lies the only clue to the spiritual world. Live the kindred life, — and the realm is open to him who so dwells in the divine atmosphere.

Bishop Brooks offers an ideal that may well be translated into a standard for every life in the words —

"The life of the Christ so far as it was public was comprised within three years and a few months. For that the previous thirty years had been a preparation. During all that time He was receiving instruction from those exalted angels who inspired him with zeal and love for His mission. He was a constant communer with the world of spirit, and was the more able to drink in their teachings that His body was no bar to His spirit."

To be "a communer with the world of spirit"! Is it not thus that this present life in the visible is linked with that life upon which we are all to enter, just beyond in the invisible; that on the faithful and earnest performance and fulfilment of all that is set before us in this world depends the degree of fitness we carry with us to enter on the realities of that world?

That the communication between that world and this is open to all who understand and fulfil the conditions is beyond question; but it is a matter of spirituality of life, of high achievement in essential qualities, rather than of phenomena. It is only by the knowledge and practice of psychic laws that this communion may become definite to the intellectual perception.

But is there any difference, it may be asked, between spiritual perception and psychic knowledge? It would seem that there is. The one is intuitive; the other as intellectual as the science of numbers. That holy men of all ages have had the open communion with the spiritual world, that they have been in touch with divine forces, there can be no

doubt; but it has been left for the present
age to formulate the spiritual laws and apprehend them as psychic science. The man who
never heard of Newton, or of the law of gravitation, is as much subject to its effects as the
savant; but he is ignorantly and blindly — not
intelligently — subject to the law.

There are many persons who are curious
rather than interested in all that pertains to
the life beyond, and who, knowing little and car-
ing less for that spirituality of life which alone
makes possible the sweet and constant communion between the Seen and the Unseen, go
to a " medium " as they would go to the theatre.
They go for a sensation, a phenomenon, and
if they do not experience this, are not backward in denouncing the possible communication, and even in denying all belief in a future
life. Communion with a friend in the Unseen,
while under favorable conditions it may assume a definite form of appeal to the sight
or hearing by means of a medium, is by no
means limited to some chance hour thus taken
at intervals. It is a matter of mutual compre-

hension and sympathy, — of spirit to spirit, — just as is the companionship and communion of life. It is, so to speak, an achievement of one's whole soul, in solitude and in silence, in its conscious and unerring recognition of the invisible and the divine. It is the end, not the immediate reward, that is the true object of quest in life. To set one's heart

> "upon the goal,
> Not on the prize,"

is the true attitude of mind. All the powers of nature, all the powers of the universe, are plastic to the force of thought. In thought is the spiritual power to act on conditions. To enlarge and elevate life to the plane of thought, to the recognition of divine purposes, to enter into harmony with these, — in this atmosphere alone may one come, not "to compete or strive," but to be enabled to so live as those spirits

> "With whom the stars connive
> To work their will."

The world is fast approaching the plane whereon the higher forces of nature hold sway. The old order changeth. All the mechanism of life is to be more swift, more subtile, more responsive. The slow and clumsy processes of the past are rapidly fading away, and the finer forces take their place. We do not now fill lamps, or even strike matches and light the gas; we turn the key, and, presto! the room is flooded with electric light. The time is close at hand when the endless manual labor of a large correspondence will be superseded by thought transference. The steam-engine gives place to the electric motor.

As with the finer and more subtile natural forces, so with the spiritual. Love and service — a loving service — is the finest expression life can assume. Generosity is a luxury even before it is a virtue. He who has it in his power to oblige another, he it is who tastes the diviner richness of life.

Love and service, — in these is found the preparation for the life beyond. In the perpetual angelic communion is found the energy which radiates in service and in love. Let these two elements enter into every experience, informing it with joy and love and peace and exaltation, and life shall take on new significances and deeper richness.

For man is created for the higher, not for the lower life. When he lives below his moral ideals, he is out of his habitat, — as a bird would be in the water, or a fish in the air. He was created for a spiritual atmosphere, and only in that does he realize his true being.

The year of 1897 dawns in brilliancy of radiant promise. Psychical research and scientific experiment and demonstration are serving religious truth. Science is revealing powers of nature, — higher forces hitherto unsuspected. The marvellous X-ray, that is even promising to enable the blind to see, and, what is perhaps more marvellous, is revealing those high vibrations of the luminiferous ether which convey that force we call thought from mind to mind without the intervention of the cells of the brain, — what a revelation is this ! For it is nothing short of the absolute demonstration of spiritual communication. It explains how thought leaps from spirit to spirit, transcending the mental mechanism, showing a process more delicate, more subtile, than were the marvels of the mind that had heretofore been known.

One reason why there has been so little, comparatively speaking, received of authentic communications from the unseen world that hold much degree of universal significance, is that the requisite conditions on this side have not been observed. Intense and devoted love has followed to the tomb, — and there it has been stayed. Devoted love has made keen the anguish of grief, but it has not possessed immediate faith. At the best, it has found what solace it might in the conviction of re-union after death, but it has held no immedi-ate convictions of satisfactory communication now and here. Theology has looked upon it as a false and vain idea; the so-called spiritualist has too largely held it to be a phenomenon of occasion, and the general public have lost no time in any meditation upon the philosophy, the speculative possibilities, or the truth underlying the subject. The devotion of thought and love that has usually followed those who have gone on into the other life has, for the most part, brooded over the past, but has not demanded the present.

The year of 1897 marks a new and clearer consciousness of man's relation with the spiritual world. The Seen and the Unseen are coming into still clearer and nearer and more intimate union. The only true union is when the mortal lifts itself to the immortal; when the advancing perception of man discovers more of the higher forces of nature, and learns to avail himself of these and to adjust his life to the plane of larger development. The communion between the Seen and the Unseen is a part of that divine life which is the higher life. As the thought flashing from spirit to spirit, it is rational; as a truth in the divine order, it is to be held in reverence and trust.

"Dead? Not to thee, thou keen watcher, — not
    silent, not viewless to thee,
  Immortal still wrapped in the mortal! I, from
    the mortal set free,
  Greet thee by many clear tokens thou smilest to
    hear and to see."

The clear recognition of this communion
of spirit between the Seen and the Unseen is
one of the great features of the immediate
future in the bringing of the earthly life of
man into harmony with heavenly principles.
A vast combination of forces are working to
this result. As Kant so well says, "The
other world is not another place, but another
view." The spiritual world is about us as an
atmosphere, and it lies with ourselves to enter
into it more and more clearly and consciously,
even while our physical organism still holds us
to the physical world. The assertion that the
pure in heart shall see God is not a merely
abstract religious phrase; not one whose
affirmative significance is restricted to experiences after death, but which may be realized
now, to-day, this hour, every hour. To see
God is to see, to perceive — which is a still

higher degree of relation — the good ; to perceive and to be in touch with spiritual beings
and divine forces.   To be in and of this life is
to live, now and here, in that atmosphere of
joy, peace, and exhilaration which is heaven.

In the realm of pure ether is the significant,
the substantial world.   Here the forces are
delicate, imponderable, but infinitely more
intense in energy.   In just that proportion in
which they are more delicate and immaterial
are they more intense.   Those who inhabit
this ethereal world are embodied in the spiritual form, — in bodies electric in energy, that
never know fatigue, and which are in perfect
harmony with their environment.

To come into a knowledge of conditions
under which any satisfactory communion can
be established between those still in this world
and those in the Unseen, is to come into the
knowledge of the conditions of spiritual life ;
of that spiritualization of life through which
alone any true and significant communion is
possible.   The atmosphere through which one
in the Unseen may be enabled to draw near is

that of radiating good-will and love. "Keep
serene in mind, and have no unkind or im-
patient thoughts of any one," was the reply
that *she* gave me when I once questioned her
as to the best conditions for establishing communion between us. And now the bewildering agony that swept over me when first I
learned that she had gone to that fair country
we shall all one day see, is transfigured to
a constant sense of the sweet and radiant atmosphere in which she lives ; and reading,
study, work, social life, take on a new aspect
and a higher charm, because every joy is
doubled in this invisible but exquisite sense
of companionship.

> "Regret is dead, but love is more
>   Than in the summers that are flown;
> For I myself with these have grown
>   To something greater than before."

Psychic science may perhaps be said to have
established the fact that the life just beyond
the present one has some determinate limit,
followed by another and another in succession,
just as this life is limited by the event we call

death ; and that this next life is not nearly so
different from our own as has been conjectured.   One goes by death, not into some
vague celestial state, but into the ethereal
world, which is a counterpart of this, only
more real and more significant.   The forces
are more delicate and intense, as an electric
motor, for instance, is more intense and delicate than a steam-engine ; as turning the key
of an electric light is a more delicate and more
potent process of obtaining illumination than
to fill and light and adjust a kerosene lamp.
If a journey is to be taken, those in the ethereal
world do not need to prepare and pack trunks
and go through the drudgery of preparation
that is requisite here ; they make the journey by the motor of thought.   Life is one,
even though it be divided by the change
we call death.   It is good to see it in its
wholeness, and realize that change is not
arbitrary and startling, but is simply development.

Spirituality of life, while it may include phenomena, does not rest on any special manifes-

tations. If it never experienced these, it would know the essential truth, even though it apprehended no details, of the life beyond. For spiritual things are spiritually discerned. It is written of Stephen, "But he, being full of the Holy Ghost, looking up steadfastly to heaven, saw the glory of God." But the condition for seeing the glory of God is in that he shall be "full of the Holy Ghost," full of the Holy Spirit.

Of the life just beyond, what can more vividly present it than these words of Phillips Brooks : —

"Heaven will not be pure stagnation, not idleness, not any mere luxurious dreaming over the spiritual repose that has been safely and forever won ; but active, tireless, earnest work ; fresh, live enthusiasm for the high labors which eternity will offer. These vivid inspirations will play through our deep repose, and make it more mighty in the service of God than any feverish and unsatisfied toil of earth has ever been. The sea of glass will be mingled with fire."

The supreme truth of the present day is the fact that psychic science is steadily conquering new territory and reclaiming the vague and the unknown to the realm of rational and intelligent comprehension. Richard Hodgson, LL.D., the Secretary of the Society for Psychical Research, is now engaged in a series of researches whose results he will duly publish, and which will give to the world a clear, definite and scientifically attested knowledge of the conditions of the next life, which will be, practically, a new revelation. It has been my privilege to read these almost daily as his work has gone on; and when they are published, the work will be of as marked importance to the conduct of life as was Newton's Principia to the progress of science. These researches are revealing the location of the world we have called heaven; its place in the universe; its nature, its conditions, and the manner in which its inhabitants approach the material world and come into a knowledge of our affairs, and into communication with us. The higher knowledge of ethics is involved in this new and larger comprehension of spiritual laws.

The new discoveries of the mysteries of the ether are inseparably conjoined with new discoveries of psychic laws. The latest scientific truth formulated is that telegraphy can be accomplished without wires, the message simply transmitted by means of electric waves in the ether. Since the discovery of the Röntgen ray in the dawning of the year 1896, a vast mass of new data concerning light, electricity, and various forms of energy have revealed themselves to the untiring efforts of science. It is now known that the brain is an electric battery : with the discovery of the electric waves that permeate the ether, the process of thought transference is as clear to the understanding as the ordinary sending of a telegram by wire. When it is further realized that death is merely the emerging from the physical case that has enveloped the real body, and that the spiritual being thus liberated comes into a condition of higher life and is in touch with the higher forces of

9

nature, then how simple and natural becomes the intercommunication of mind to mind, spirit to spirit. The poet's exclamation,

" Across the world I speak to thee,"

is the mere assertion of a fact.

Of the extreme sensitiveness of this electric communication through the ether, I have become unmistakably conscious since she — who was dearest of all to me — has gone into the ethereal world. It is a literal fact that I have never appealed to her with any question, entreaty, or endearment that the response has not been swift, definite, and unmistakable. This response is made in various ways. Sometimes it is telepathic directly from her mind to my own; sometimes it is made through other persons who fulfil the matter regarding which I had appealed to her. There could be hundreds of pages filled with specific occurrences and incidents, each and all of which I could fully substantiate and corroborate to the reader, save that one's sense of the delicacy and fitness of intimate experiences hardly admits of placing such inevitably personal matters before the public. Yet — such is my serious conviction of the supreme importance of establishing the recognition of larger spiritual outlook — I have been tempted to sacrifice any sense of literary art to the higher claim of psychic truth.

The two conditions for entering into this beautiful and uplifting comprehension of the divine laws that govern the relations between the Seen and the Unseen are belief and prayer. It is prayer that lifts the soul into the ethereal region, and the command of the Christ to pray without ceasing defines the conditions of living in perpetual communion with the diviner world.

Love is not barred by death, but, rather, when the beloved has passed beyond the ethereal veil into that region which is still so near and interpenetrates all our atmosphere, then, indeed, is all affection, all friendship, all tenderness of devotion invested with new potencies. Then begins the real relation of spirit to spirit; so infinitely nearer and clearer in its mutual comprehensiveness and love that one realizes suddenly how it is life that separates and death that unites.

If the great grief that fell upon me on that radiant June morning last year — a grief that seemed to efface all possibilities of joy and to paralyze endeavor — shall have been the means of permitting me to enter on new paths of knowledge ; if it shall result in enabling my own experience to be even of the least service and comfort to others who know this supreme anguish in the death of their beloved, — shall I not give thanks that it was sent to me, even as *she*, whose life here was constantly filled with the noblest aspirations and the divinest inspirations, would also rejoice to still further serve the humanity to whose aid and betterment her life was devoted ? Ah, that exquisite and lovely and radiant presence ! that spirit so finely touched that only fine issues could await its progress ! She was one who impressed the imagination. She was indeed

"Made of spirit, and fire, and dew,"

and she always abounded in spiritual energy.
Delicate in physique, artistic in temperament,
lofty in all poetic and heroic feeling, hers was
that intense and exquisitely wrought nature
that leaves forever its haunting impress. The
pathos of her death, alone, on that far-off
island in the Pacific, lies with me "too deep
for tears;" and my only claim to the hope
and the prayer that this little story of the experiences and meditations after her death may
possibly offer some comfort to those who have
been bereaved, lies in the fact that life and
work have been made possible to me again by
the reality of my continued companionship
with her. It comes in the sense of a spiritual consciousness surrounding me like an
atmosphere.

One cannot offer mere personal impressions
as proofs of his personal convictions; but facts
established both by science and by psychical
research may be presented. Science comes
to the aid of psychic research, and the two,
working along different lines, obtain results
that harmonize and supplement each other.

For instance, psychic research has brought
to our conception the ethereal body, which
is the finer counterpart of the physical, and
has learned that all the senses save that of
taste are retained and intensified, and that
there are, also, indescribable new senses.
Now science discovers that the ether is permeated with electric waves, through which
communication can be sent to any distance,
without the slightest mechanism, — needing
only the mind of the sender and the receiver.
What is this but a spiritual communication?
And why is it not just as rational to suppose
that two minds — the one in the physical,
the one in the ethereal world — can thus
transmit messages to each other, as that a
man in Calcutta can transmit a message to
his friend in Chicago?

The ether interpenetrates all our atmosphere, and fills all interplanetary space. How
easy and even inevitable then may communication be between those in this world, or
those here and those in the one beyond
death! And in this scientific fact, so recently

discovered, lies the explanation of the process we call telepathy. This ether transmits sound waves at the rate of one hundred and ninety-two thousand miles per second. At this rate it does not take long to "put a girdle round the earth."

The ethereal world is invisible to us simply because its life is a matter of higher vibrations. The human eye cannot see beyond the limit of a vibration of eight hundred trillions per second, and the human ear is likewise limited. So that all life in a higher state of vibration than this is invisible and inaudible. There is a field of tremendous forces in this upper region, which science is just beginning to apprehend. "The air is full of miracles," says a recent authority. "The certainty is, strange things are coming, and coming soon."

The ethereal world was open to Jesus because he lived the life of spirituality. In proportion as one achieves this, does the realm just beyond grow clearer. In this spiritual perspective the experiences common to all are seen in their truer values. One

comes to perceive that the only enduring realities are the moral victories which his higher
nature gains over the lower.   He discovers
that external conditions are but the transitory
scenery through which he is passing, and hold
no permanent power for good or for ill over
his life.

The establishment of definite, recognized,
and intelligent communication between the
seen and the unseen would make a new era
in the development of the race.   To reject the
idea as irreverent is as idle as it would be to
deprecate establishing social relations with a
neighboring city or continent.   The advantage
would be an infinite illumination in all arts
and inventions that have to do with the
higher forces of nature : in infinite comfort,
and in the absolute demonstration of personal
immortality.   Life would be exalted and en-
nobled.   As heaven is a condition, and not
a place, it is entered simply by the achievement of that spirituality which fits one for
its diviner air, and enables him to affirm :
" Thou hast made known to me the ways

of life; Thou shalt fill me full of joy with Thy countenance." Thus shall life be radiant, joyful, and abound in spiritual energy, and into its daily experiences shall enter the King of Glory.

THE DEEPER MEANING OF THE HOUR.

It seems to me natural, judging by my own feeling of what I should be impelled to do, that spirits should desire to communicate with their friends on earth.

KATE FIELD.

During the conjunction of body and soul, nature orders the one to obey and the other to command. Which of these two characters is most suitable to the Divine Being, or to that which is mortal? Are you not sensible that the divine is only capable of commanding, and what is mortal is only worthy of obedience?

THE PHAEDON OF PLATO.

"Man is a duality, consisting of an organized spiritual form, evolved coincidently with and permeating the physical body, and having corresponding organs and developments. Death is the separation of this duality, and effects no change in the spirit, morally or intellectually."

THE DEEPER MEANING OF THE HOUR.

And, oh, the wonder and the power,
The deeper meaning of the hour!

EMERSON.

THE nature of intercommunication between the two worlds of the Seen and the Unseen falls into the two phases of the telepathic and the mediumistic, — the first being that which one may achieve personally, and the second that which he attains through a psychic. To allude to the professional medium is to invite incredulity, distrust, and ridicule on the part of a large number of intelligent and cultivated people ; and realizing this, I only venture to do so by earnestly entreating the reader to divest himself of any prejudice or adverse preconceptions he may hold, and judge on its merits the vast quantity of new data before

the world at the present time. It is to be at
once conceded that there is much deliberate
and intentional fraud, much unconscious and
unintentional delusion, under the phase of
mediumship. But as it is not with that
which is false and ignorant that we have to
do, it is not worth while to waste energy over
its discussion or its refutation. Error has no
tenure on life, and truth is eternal.

> " Get but the truth once uttered, and 't is like
>   A star new-born that drops into its place
>   And which, once circling in the placid round,
>   Not all the tumults of the earth can shake."

Aside from conscious deception or unconscious delusion, there is a vast and an increasing amount of evidence of communication
between those who have passed through the
change called death and those still in the
physical body, which is as incontrovertible as
any other actual occurrences in life.

The larger portion of the long communications from *her* — my beloved friend whose
transition to the other life has seemed to so

open its nature to me — are impossible to
relate here in full for two reasons. One,
which is sufficiently obvious to every one, is
in the inevitable personalities that are involved,
and also that the telepathic portions of it,
while convincing to myself, are, by their very
nature, so subtile and involved with the most intimate inner life, as to render narration almost
impossible; while, on the other hand, the
hundreds of pages of definite, objective communications, written through the hand of the
medium, are the property, so to speak, of the
Psychical Society, and it is not permitted to
make them public until the authorized Pro-
ceedings are published. A group of learned
men, scholars and scientists, are devoting themselves earnestly to this work of psychic research; they permit very few to hold any
séance with the medium under their control;
and whoever enjoys this privilege must re-
spect their conditions. In the present desire
to offer to the reader testimony to the truth
which I hold to be of the supremest importance, I would even sacrifice much of the

reserve which usually invests intimate personal experiences, for the sake of offering the
due support of facts to the argument. In
any case, however, fidelity to the trust im-
posed by the Society forbids, as my experiences through their medium are their records
to be used among their data. There have been
evidential phenomena of the most convincing
character : personal experiences of my own,
when alone in my own room, in connection
with the reading of certain books and the
writing of certain matters, with a conviction
on my part of her presence, have been written
by her the next day (through the hand of the
medium) to Dr. Hodgson, who submitted to
me the assertions made, to be verified or
denied. It is with an almost incredulous
amazement that I have read many of these, —
depicting in detail movements and work of my
own, on the preceding day, when entirely
alone in my own rooms. It was impossible
to deny that some super-normal intelligence —
which had not only noted my outward acts,
but read and understood my thoughts — had

companioned me, unseen and unheard, but
none the less real ; and then had registered,
through the hand of the medium, facts and
thought-currents entirely unknown to her and
to the Secretary, Dr. Hodgson. The theory
of clairvoyance on the part of the medium
does not cover the ground, which largely involved that of my own mental life, as well as
outward actions. The theory that my own
subliminal self went out to this psychic and
wrote through her, involves an equal or a
greater mystery, even, than the more simple
one, that my friend, as a spiritual being, was
in my room and saw and heard what she wrote
that she did. It is less mysterious that the
spiritual body when liberated by death from
its physical case may see, hear, and record
through a mediumistic instrument certain occurrences, than it is that the spiritual self, while
still conjoined to its physical body, can go out
and do this. The latter is possible, but it is
certainly more complicated than the former.
Again, my proof that the communications
signed with the name of my friend were truly

10

from her, lies in that they have narrated many
things totally unknown to me, or to the
psychic, but which I have afterward learned,
from persons involved, to be explicitly true.
My proof lies also — and this is, to myself,
one even more potent — in the absolute individuality of the very essence of the communications; turns of expression; characteristic
feelings and sentiments: the subtile, potent,
and utterly unmistakable flavor of her own
very strong and decided nature. At one time
I had been looking over several boxes of her
books and papers, and found that she had, as
we are all apt to do, saved much that had
become worthless. To a friend who chanced
to come, I had remarked, in reference to these
accumulations, that she had a fatal habit of
saving things. In a few days I went again
for a sitting with the psychic. *She* came and
among many other things wrote: "Yes, I
saved a great deal too much. I see it was always a fault of mine to do so." Could there
be any doubt that she heard my remark and
thus replied? If it be suggested that my own

subjective self controlled the medium and wrote this, it must be remembered that a large proportion of these communications have been of things I did not know, but afterward verified.

In offering any evidential data as authoritative testimony, however, one should either be prepared to submit it *in toto,* or else refrain altogether. As has been said, it is impossible here to do this, for even were I to entirely sacrifice all natural reserve on intimate personal matters, I am not permitted to use matter, at present, obtained under the auspices and by the invaluable courtesy of the Society for Psychical Research, through the personal consent of its Secretary, Dr. Hodgson. This restriction is one that time will remove, and I cannot refrain from the hope that at a future period I may venture to offer in another volume matter now inevitably withheld.

The intercourse that is now so unmistakably established between *her* and myself owes much of its success to the fact that

she possessed strong psychic power. The
instrument known as "Planchette" wrote
under her hand in so remarkable a manner
that she compiled a little book of these
communications, which was published under
the title of "Planchette's Diary." The
volume is now out of print, but from my
own copy I extract the record of one sitting. The "Mr. and Mrs. F." referred to
are Rev. O. B. and Mrs. Frothingham. The
record runs:—

"We dined to-day with Mr. and Mrs. F.,
and in the evening had a long and very interesting *séance* with Planchette in the presence of half a dozen persons. Planchette
made a correct report of the physical condition of Mr. F.'s nearest relative, of whom
I knew nothing; gave an admirable analysis
of Mr. F.'s character; referred to the nature
of his ancestry, of which I was ignorant;
when questioned about Shakespeare, Fanny
Kemble, and Edwin Booth, gave clever criti-
cisms thereon, and was witty as well as wise.
This was the verdict of those assembled, who

pronounced Planchette 'to be very singular indeed.'

"The *séance* was too personal for the public eye. Planchette would communicate with no one but Mr. F., and expressed the greatest desire that he should himself experiment with the board for the purpose of investigation, 'because,' argued Planchette, 'he has a clear head, and if he once believes, he will not hesitate to promulgate the truth that is, in one form or another, as old as the hills.'

"Mr. F. manifested a great deal of interest. Planchette wrote twenty-six long pages."

On another date she recorded: —

". . . None of us were Spiritualists, and we naturally speculated upon the phenomena; whereupon Planchette wrote: 'Do believe in the reality of Spiritualism. How can you doubt the truth of these phenomena? How can your mind control when so much is written that you dream not of? Soon you will discriminate, and the influences around you are so fine that you will obtain exceeding comfort from so-called Planchette.'"

During her life here she was not a "Spiritualist" in the accepted sense, but her mind was too hospitable to progress for her to oppose any wall of prejudice to new phases of knowledge. In a final chapter of theories regarding the phenomenon of the Planchette writing, she says: —

. . . "It behooves me to say that I am not a Spiritualist; nevertheless, I have no prejudice whatever against a belief in spiritual communion. If we are endowed with immortal souls, and preserve our individuality in another existence, it seems to me natural, judging by my own feeling of what I should be impelled to do, that spirits should desire to communicate with their friends on earth. There is no known law against such a proceeding, and there *may* be a law in support of it.

"The Bible teems with supernatural visitations, and if they are possible at one time, who shall say they are impossible at another? From our cradles we are taught to believe in the ministering of angels, and literature abounds in allusions to this belief.

" 'Millions of spiritual creatures walk the earth
Unseen, both when we wake and when we sleep,'

says Milton, and Sir Thomas Browne is not
a whit less confident of the fact. 'I do
think,' reasons the author of 'Religio Medici,'
'that many mysteries ascribed to our own
inventions have been the courteous revela-
tions of spirits.' . . .

"From the sensations undergone while
using Planchette I am inclined to believe
myself to be under the influence of a won-
derfully subtle magnetic fluid. Whence it
comes is the important question."

These extracts from her own record of
experiences with Planchette reveal her delicate susceptibility to psychic influences and
her mental receptivity to the unknown; and
these characteristics are, one may well believe,
potent factors in the very remarkable success
attending her establishment of communication
from the Unseen to this world.

By the kindness of Mrs. Mabel Loomis
Todd and other friends I had been enabled to
follow her outward experiences up to the very
moment of her leaving this world. Telling her

this, and asking her some questions to which she clearly replied, I begged her to take up the story from the moment of her conscious waking in the other life. She did so, and told me (writing through the hand of the medium) that her first consciousness in the other world was that of standing on the floor in the room in which her body lay. Her father and mother were beside her; and her mother, calling her by name, said, "Come, my child, have no fear," and she then went away with them and joined other near relatives.

"But tell me," I entreated, "of your life in the new conditions."

"It is very simple and natural," she replied; "I live in a house with my father and mother. My brother is here. He is grown up now, and is a man. I read and study and cultivate my mind. I hear beautiful music and noble lectures, and enjoy art in the drama and in paintings. I lecture, myself, and my audiences are far more intelligent and clear-headed than they were in your world. I can travel without any fatigue, and, as I have told you, the sensation of flying through the air is delicious."

" Can you really hear me when I call to you ? " I inquired.

" Yes," she replied, " and I almost always come. If you will speak aloud, very slowly and distinctly, with about five seconds between each word, I can hear you perfectly."

In my rooms I have a large number of her photographs, taken from the time she was a child up to the year of her death, and I asked her which one of these she looked the most like in her new life.

" The one with the flowers," she replied, — which was one taken in her early twenties, showing a very spirited and delicate face, at about the same time that the portrait was taken of which a reproduction forms the frontispiece of this volume.

At another time she wrote : —

" Dear ——, you have no idea of the happiness of this world. I could not begin to express to you the sense of freedom and exhilaration that I feel."

The psychical communion that has seemed to exist between us falls into three general divisions: that which, in the years before we ever met, attracted my mind to dwell upon her and fascinated my imagination; that which was always experienced during the last fifteen years of her life here, after we met; and that which has attended this one year after her death. She was a great traveller while here, and our correspondence during her long journeys — to Europe, to the far West, to Alaska, and at last to Honolulu — reveals countless instances of letters crossing with almost identical thoughts, desires, or expressions, attesting the telepathic communication between us even then.

All this is but preliminary to the one salient and supreme truth that may easily be deduced from it, — the unmistakable assurance of the persistence of identity in the life of the spirit, in the body and out of the body. All our social life in this world is spiritual life; all our loves and friendships are of the spirit, — certainly not of the body. *The nature of the spiritual being which temporarily inhabits a physical body in the physical world, is in no wise altered by the event of death, which liberates it from this physical case.* When liberated, it enters on life in the ethereal world, which is the corresponding counterpart of life in this world. If we could clearly comprehend what life would be now with the entire elimination of all physical demands, we should approach the comprehension of what the life on the next higher plane must be. Take away all that ministers to the physical needs ; imagine beginning the day without care for the body, or for a thousand purely transient and material interests that beset us here, and that one is thus left free for the higher thought, for purely mental and spiritual occupations. Imagine communication carried on, not by letters and telegrams, but by the instant flight of thought ; imagine travelling to be a matter of will and instant performance rather than an affair demanding preparation in detail, as with us : imagine a realm, indeed, where all the clumsy processes of material life are eliminated, and where the law of thought, controlling vibrations, is understood and acted upon, and to some degree can we thus achieve some comprehension of the nature of life in the ethereal world.

The one point of supreme importance, however, in the establishment of the truth of intercommunication between the Seen and the Unseen is that it enters into our present daily life, uplifting and enlightening it. The spiritual being, temporarily inhabiting his physical body, realizes himself as an immortal being whose responsibility it is to fill the days with significant experiences. The choice rests with one's self entirely. It may seem a thing largely and almost inevitably dependent on circumstances, but it is not ; for thought is greater than circumstance or event, and dominates them. Significance or insignificance in the quality of life is, like good or evil, a matter of personal choice with the individual. It is possible to eliminate the inane hours and make every day tell in its purposes of fulfilment. Nor is this possibility restricted to the city dweller, in the heart of all that which is finest in art, literature, and ethics. It is a matter of individual choice rather than that of individual opportunity. Dante advised that men eat angels' food, and be not content with the kind of food that they share with the brutes. The angels' food abounds, whether in city or in country. It is not only in art; it is in literature, that can always be obtained, and it is in the air. Man does not live by bread alone. He lives by every word that proceedeth out of the mouth of God; that is to say, by every inspiration that in some finer way than by word or sign enters into his inner consciousness.

There can be a realization of that finer world interpenetrating that in which we live. Its ether is in the atmosphere we breathe. It is the world of reality, of force, of vividness, of power. Now it is not only they who have passed on beyond the things of sense who live in this world, but it is one in which the higher self, the ethereal organism, may live, even before it leaves the body. Everything in this natural world has its spiritual or ethereal counterpart. Nature perpetuates herself in more delicate yet more potent forms. The ethereal body which man assumes at death is a counterpart of the body here; it has the same form, only that it is etherealized. It is not less, but more real. It has to do with a higher range of correspondences. It is an inhabitant of a more important plane of life. Science has demonstrated the existence of the finer atmospheric ether in which this finer body lives and moves. There is a world touching and mingling with ours in which lie the springs of power. Most people live, sometimes, and fragmentarily, in this world. They recognize moments, hours, days, when event and sequence become rhythmic, when the vision shines clear and the voice is heard. Now if it be possible to so live one day in the year, it is possible to so live three hundred and sixty-five days in a year. If it be possible for one hour a day, it is possible for twenty-four hours. This intensity and exaltation constantly records its impress on the air, — that is, in this finer ethereal world. The deed is the outward and momentary expression ; the motive and purpose are the inner and permanent elements that build up life on the invisible side. One who holds his purpose true to this higher end of life is creating new conditions that will ultimately transform all circumstances. There is no limit to that which he may accomplish. He holds the key to the unlimited stores of energy.

All aims of a high character bring into being their own ways and means. Every noble purpose holds its own right of way.

Nothing conduces more to the holding of the days to a standard of significance than the quiet half-hour alone at night just before retiring. It is possible to absolutely create the next day in this time of silent, concentrated energy. Thought shapes and controls everything. Events are plastic to its stamp. The succeeding day may be created on the preceding night, — may be forged out of love, harmony, and energy. Any writer may experience the almost miraculous results of this form of auto-suggestion. Any business man may redeem his affairs from entanglement and disorder and peril, by a silent half-hour alone at night, when in thought he shall understand and bring them to order, harmony, and prosperous conduct. Thoughts not only "let us into realities," as Emerson truly says, but they magnetize the elements. The man whose affairs are in danger may, by mental action, summon to his aid the individual, or the capital, or the aid in any way required. The artist can thus achieve the power of creation or of attracting orders and sales; the writer can decide what he will produce, and can draw from the infinite potency of the ethereal world the conceptions and the expression required. Financial aid can be drawn. As for money, there is money enough; the only problem is to learn how to touch and control financial currents.

It is this ethereal world which is the World Beautiful, — the world in which all potencies are stored, from which every form of progress, success, and happiness can be drawn. It is the world wherein all who live the life of significance may dwell, and thus may one so live that he will constantly manifest the Divine.

The spirit's progress is as much a concern of life here as it is hereafter. This progress is, as an ancient writer has truly said, " a process of regeneration, typified by crucifixion and resurrection. The old is crucified ; the new is raised up to live a spiritual and holy life. In the life of spiritual progress there should be no stagnation, no paralysis. It should be a growth and a daily adaptation of knowledge ; a repression of the earthly ; a development of the spiritual and heavenly ; a lifelong struggle with self ; an ever-widening grasp of Divine truth." It is not merely man's privilege, but his present personal duty, in this present state of existence to live the ideal life. Perfection is no impossible dream, though no mortal has yet ever fully realized it. The command of Jesus, " Be ye perfect, even as your Father in heaven is perfect," is just as binding as a moral law as are the Ten Commandments or the Sermon on the Mount. It

11

is the simple duty of every human being to be honest, just, truthful, diligent, kind. Furthermore, it is as absolutely his duty to be considerate of each and all with whom he comes in direct and close or in incidental and accidental contact; to be courteous; to be hospitable to the best endeavors of every one else, and see people at their best always, and not at their worst; to be generous, and — higher than all and inclusive of all — to be loving. To radiate a sunny sweetness and love to every one, as the rose radiates its color and fragrance, is the normal condition of living. Anything below this is abnormal. The ideal life is the normal life. "To err is human?" Not in the least. To err is *inhuman.* When the individual errs, he does that which, as a spiritual being, made in the likeness of the heavenly, he has no business to do. He is not an animal; he is a man. He is a divine being, whose true environment is the divine world. Now the divine world is not a mere phrase of rhetoric that has no meaning; it is the most real and the most positive thing in the universe. It has even its location in that finer ether which pervades the outer air. This finer ether is, undoubtedly, the spiritual atmosphere, — the air breathed by those who have gone out from the body into the ethereal world. The ethereal form is probably so fashioned as to breathe this ethereal air, this finer ether which science has discovered and registered. We, who are potentially the ethereal inhabitants of the ethereal world, are already, in our spiritual natures, related to it, and so far as we live in the spirit we live in the spiritual world, in touch with spiritual forces, and companioned by spiritual beings. Into this world evil cannot enter. When we do evil, we separate ourselves from this realm, where it is not only our privilege, but our duty, to live. We are suddenly thrust out from it because we have allied ourselves with conditions that cannot enter it. This truth is typically illustrated on the physical plane of life. Let the educated and cultivated man whose society has been that of cultivated and lovely people suddenly fall into sin, into crime, into anything base and low, and by an unwritten law he is thrust outside the social companionship of high and beautiful life. Only a gentleman can be the associate of gentlemen. Only one who lives the spiritual life of peace, love, sweetness, exaltation, on the basis of truth, justice, and honesty, can be the associate, can have the companionship of spiritual presences. There may be pity, there may be the desire on the part of the higher to help and uplift the lower; but *until* the lower *is* uplifted, he cannot have on easy, equal terms the companionship of the higher nature.

And to so great a degree is it true that " Evil is wrought by want of thought." The thoughtless word is spoken, and the offender explains that he meant no harm, but that he did n't think. But here is just the point. It is his business to think! For what other conceivable purpose was he formed in the heavenly image and given a rational mind? What is he in the world for? To think is his initial duty.

Now it may not be in the nature of a luxury for a man to sit down with himself and accuse his inner life of having been recreant to its divine trusts. But it is often far more wholesome for our moral progress to accuse than to excuse ourselves. One sees suddenly that his life is all in an entanglement of disasters. What disturbances have entered? What has deflected the magnetic needle from pointing the true cause? Some wrong-doing of his own. There can be no possible doubt of it. Let him recognize it fully and fairly ; let him overcome it in spirit, atone for it in any way possible on the outward plane. Let him by prayer and intercession regain his place in the spiritual companionship of the ethereal world. To this end an external renewal will often contribute, as corresponding to the internal. There is moral efficacy in a complete change of costume and environment, of seeking new elements in light, bloom, color, fragrance, in music, poetry, and art. " Behold, I make all things new " is a practical formula, for a change in vibrations can reconstruct all existing states. That thought can entirely transform the atomic vibrations is a scientific fact. By grasping this law man may learn to control all his outer circumstances and render them the harmonious manifestation of his spiritual state. The formula is simple. Atoms, whose combinations make every existing thing, are the result of vibrations; vibrations are under the direct control of thought.

The French savant, M. Desertis, writing of the entrance into the new life, says:—

"True, appallingly true, is the fact of judgment to come, and inexorable as fate its coming. For it is the revealing of what we *are*, that birth into spirit life, disclosing under rigid law the qualities of the true self; it is a strictly continuous process, and he who may desire to know how he will appear in that new life has only to think how he would be ashamed to go among the highest, noblest men and women with all his thoughts spoken aloud as each arises in his mind, for that is the state he has to enter into. Fair as a sculptor's dream, unstained by greed or malice, will show the souls of some of earth's humblest, not because they are rewarded for having been poor, but because they *are* strong and pure and brave and true ; while terrible will be the awakening of those enervated by materiality, or who have thought that devotion to a creed can cover the want of that love for man which works unselfishly for the higher good."

The new discoveries of science throw a high illumination on psychic truth. The wildest dream of the magician of the Middle Ages never essayed to compass a more marvellous feat than is suggested by one of the recent experiments in electrical science on the human body. Wonderful as is the phenomenon of the X ray, this latest discovery surpasses that. The Roentgen ray directed to the human body reveals the bones ; but it is now found that minute globules of electricity can be swallowed with the effect of making the entire body transparent. If there is an opaque spot, it is because that it locates some disease or defect. If there is perfect health, there is perfect transparency. In proportion as there is not this transparence is the defective physical condition. This new discovery seems to correspond on the physical plane with the aspects of spiritual life on the spiritual plane. The ethereal body expresses the quality of spiritual life, and this life will begin with just that state to which one has attained, — with just the degree he has achieved when the transition from this world to the other comes. How this scientific truth corresponds with the spiritual truth expressed in the words, "God is light, and in Him is no darkness at all"! Because He is perfect and without sin, there is in Him no darkness. In proportion as our own spiritual natures are without sin, so are they illuminated. In proportion as the physical body is without disease, so is it transparent. How these truths attest the correspondence between physical and spiritual states!

Milton expresses the same truth in the lines: —

"For God is light and never but in unapproached
        light,
Dwelt from Eternity."

Alfred Russel Wallace, F. R. S., concisely states the nature of man in the words : —

"Man is a duality consisting of an organized spiritual form, evolved coincidently with and permeating the physical body, and having corresponding organs and developments. Death is the separation of this duality, and effects no change in the spirit, morally or intellectually.

"Progressive evolution of the intellectual and moral natures is the destiny of individuals : the knowledge, attainments, and experience of earth life forming the basis of spirit life."

Looking backward over past ages, the observer of the panorama of history realizes how infinitely finer is the civilization on the eve of the twentieth century than ever before. The age of the material is not passed, but the age of spirit has certainly begun. The supremacy of spirit is everywhere asserted; more and more is humanity realizing that material things are the servants of spiritual forces, and that the spiritual achievement is the *raison d'être* of embodied existence.

For instance, the true view of physical life is as a means, not as an end. The body is clothed, fed, refreshed variously; not because food and clothing are an end, *per se,* but because it is the instrument of the spirit, and in order that it may accomplish its work, it must be kept in good condition. Here is just the point where the higher life differentiates from the lower life. The higher asserts the supremacy of the spirit as the real man, whose works and ways are of significance, and uses the material things as tools to its accomplishments. The real man is one and the same in this life, or in what we call the other life. He persists. He casts off the physical body, and emerges into a realm of higher and finer forces. This life is very clumsy compared with that. The amount of impedimenta one must drag about with him when he travels, and even to some extent when he merely goes out for business, or visits, is while here unavoidable; but the mere fact of being free from the care of the body liberates the real man, as is easily seen, from a host of encumbrances. Not but that these have their use. It is not he who denies and deserts, but he who is nobly true to his present trust who is best prepared for the next step. Life may be a burden, but its cure is not found in suicide. Its richer results lie in experience, and all the pursuits and combinations of affairs furnish this experience. After this is gained, the rudiments and factors may fall off. They are of no further consequence; but to deny their use is a fatal error. He is best prepared to enter on the life just beyond death who has lived here in the fullest and noblest way; who has held the largest relations with this life on the one side, and with all the divine life on the other.

Thus, to be conscious, constantly conscious, of one's relations with the ethereal life is to elevate and enlarge and ennoble every relation with this part of life. To be conscious of the presence, the companionship, the communion, telepathically, of spirit to spirit, is to possess a spring of invigoration and of exhilaration that is unfailing. When one possesses this consciousness he has happiness. Temporary ills and accidents cannot trouble or depress him, for he realizes that he is a spiritual being, living in a spiritual world. The present civilization is evolved to that degree that the next step is to lay hold in a clear and comprehensive perception of this unseen world and its higher forces. Each new discovery and application of higher laws brings it nearer. Such discoveries as those of the Roentgen ray, of globules of electricity, which, when swallowed, render the body transparent, are bringing us to the very confines of that ethereal realm which is the corresponding hemisphere to this life on earth. The two are inter-related, and the separation is overcome in just the degree to which man achieves spirituality of life.

Nor should the term "Spiritualism" be held in intellectual disrepute. All of us who believe in God and immortality accept a part of its significance by that very belief, and the special differentiation in the belief of the present communication between the two worlds is one that is more and more increasing its hold on thoughtful people. Aside from this, however, there are certain important significances in the faith that there is no break in the continuity of life which react on conduct here and now. To realize one's essential and individual life as entirely separated from the physical body is to realize the necessity of intellectual culture, of moral achievement, as the only foundation for happiness.

"He who believes that just in proportion as he indulges in passion or selfishness, or the exclusive pursuit of wealth, and neglects to cultivate the affections and the varied powers of his mind, so does he inevitably prepare for himself misery in a world where there are no physical wants to provide for, no occupations but those having for their object social and intellectual and spiritual progress, — such an one is impelled toward pure, high, sympathetic life by motives far stronger than either the teachings of religion or philosophy can supply. He dreads to give way to passion or to falsehood, to selfishness or to a life of luxurious physical enjoyment, because he knows the inevitable misery of such habits, necessitating the long struggle to develop new and higher faculties. He who knows the realities of the future existence knows that happiness **or** misery will be directly dependent on the mental fabric we construct by our thoughts and words and actions daily."

Such a philosophy as this is its own incentive to the constant culture of character; and not only in view of happiness that we are able to create for ourselves after the transition to the next life, but in view of the happiness here and now. Each year is creating the future year; each day creates to-morrow; each hour is influencing the succeeding one. The apostle has a phrase of sowing to the spirit and reaping the fruits of the spirit, and of sowing to the flesh, and of the flesh reaping corruption. To live in serenity, in poise, in harmony, love, and sweetness is to sow to the spirit, and of the spirit reap like fruits. It is to produce beautiful and favorable conditions. It is to live in that serene activity of " without haste, without rest," which is a very different thing from a frantic and chaotic haste. To fall into a nervous flurry and clamor, to sink into selfish greed, or impatience, or hatred, or distrust, is to sow to the flesh, and of the flesh reap corruption in ill-advised action, in unfortunate circumstances, in discordant conditions.

Life itself, the quality of life, daily, in its simple, natural relations, is the most important thing in the world. It is far more important than any special work or achievement can possibly be. " If we live truly, we shall see truly."

There is an infinite expansion possible to time that reverses its power, substituting quality for quantity. In the state of poise, serenity, and exaltation all accomplishment is easy. An hour shall concentrate in itself the energies of a day. A day shall do the work of a week. It is not time that matters, but degree ; to keep one's self in spiritual harmony, — this is to conquer and prevail. There is no purpose served in flying to pieces because of unforeseen obstacles and interruptions. It is not these that count, or affect to much extent the desired accomplishment, but the spirit in which they are met. Hindrances are, to be sure, of various orders, and not every one is a divine call. One must discriminate ; when the unforeseen interruption *is* a divine call, when it is chiefly a duty, the result will take care of itself. Minutes will do the work of months.

The season of achievement is not limited by the sojourn in this part of life. This state is an experimental one. We are learning *how* to live. If one cultivates his mind, his character, his higher nature, he is getting out of life its best purposes, and doing the will of his Father who is heaven. This is the essential thing : other matters are accidental and contingent.

The spiritual philosophy of life conceives it in its wholeness from this standpoint. The future is not a system of arbitrary rewards and retributions, but the natural and inevitable results of the present. Each one creates his future. Its joy or its sorrow is within his own power and option. This conviction makes each day and hour its own responsibility, but its own joy and promise as well. Let one sow to the spirit, and of the spirit reap love, joy, and peace.

The highest quality of communion between the two worlds is that which is purely spiritual, moulding thought and inciting to higher purposes. A new and a larger revelation of the divine laws which govern the development of the spirit began in a crude and humble way with that phenomenon known as the " Rochester rappings." It began with this physical phenomenon appealing to the physical senses. The intercourse has progressed in its nature and quality during its half-century of existence, and will continue to grow finer and more significant just in proportion as the mind grows more receptive to higher truth. No one can receive beyond the degree that he is prepared to recognize. In the relative im-

12

portance of intercommunication between the two worlds, mere phenomenon is of the least importance. It had its place in arresting attention; but the scientific investigation now being carried on by the Psychical Society will offer to the world results which appeal to the most intelligent and thoughtful people with convincing persuasion and the invincible logic of truth.

The question has been asked as to whether every person can hold telepathic communion with those in the Unseen. It might, doubtless, be truly answered that every person does, although comparatively few may be conscious of it. Its intelligent consciousness is a question of the development of the spiritual faculties. These may be so trained as to grow more and more sensitive to the higher vibrations, as a musician's ear, by training, is more delicately sensitive to a more extensive range of vibration than is the untrained ear.

One comes back, however, to the one truth that the development of spiritual faculties is based on the moral life, on the simple fidelity to truth, generosity, and ideal purpose. One very exalted spirit who has given much instruction to the Psychical Society through a recognized medium, wrote : —

"The holding of a narrow, cold, dogmatic creed, in all its rigid, lifeless literalism, cramps the soul, dwarfs its spirituality, and clogs its progress. We call you to a spiritualized religion. We call you from the dead formalism, the lifeless, loveless literalism of the past, to a religion of spiritualized truth, to the lovely symbolism of angel teaching, to the higher planes of spirit, when the material finds no place and the formal dogmatism of the past is forever gone. The Divine aid will minister to all who pray for it."

Living daily, hourly, in this spirit, the telepathic intercourse with those in the life beyond will be developed to such a degree as to form the familiar intercourse of perpetual companionship. The daily life will become transfigured in this exaltation and joy, and one can but exclaim with Emerson, that mystic seer and poet, —

" And, oh, the wonder of the power,
  The deeper meaning of the hour! "

For in this revelation of deeper meaning shall the discords and perplexities of life flee away like shadows. It shall be seen that the spiritual being carries on into the next stage of existence that which he has here transmuted into his experience, and that there is thus the highest incentive to live daily as seeing Him who is invisible, and beholding, as in vision, the Mount of Transfiguration.

THE END.

TWENTIETH THOUSAND.

THE WORLD BEAUTIFUL.

(FIRST SERIES.)

BY LILIAN WHITING.

16mo. Cloth. Price, $1.00. White and Gold, $1.25.

No one can read it through without feeling himself the better and richer and happier for having done so. — *The Independent.*

There is in its pages such a strong assertion of the possible supremacy of the spiritual over the physical if only the effort is made ; such an affirmation of the happiness which results from such a supremacy ; such an inspiration to all who desire to live the higher life ; and withal an optimism that, in this day and generation of pessimism, is above and beyond all things refreshing and helpful, it is no wonder that struggling humanity gives such a work warm welcome. — *Toledo Blade.*

There is no sermonizing upon either right or wrong ; she lives, and for the time causes us to live, in a world either actually or potentially beautiful. — *Boston Budget.*

There is an agreeable unity in the essays. While varied and differenced, they are yet one in their theme and tenor,—the world beautiful which we create for ourselves and others by our generous and high-thoughted activities. The publishers have given these notable essays a worthy setting ; they have made a dainty and beautiful volume ; and no one can do a friend a better service than to get the book and send it to him without delay. — *Prof. Louis J Block, in the Philosophical Journal.*

The five essays that make up this volume are on that high plane of living and thinking for which Lilian Whiting has been remarkable from the dawn of her bright career. Few women have produced a book so full of the choicest ethical ideas set forth in language so pure and elevated that no right-minded person can fail to find a genuine attraction on every page. — *Frances E. Willard.*

In "The World Beautiful" Lilian Whiting discusses, with clairvoyant cleverness and marked acumen, all the topics that engage the earnest thought of advanced, broad-minded men and women, and it is a hive of garnered sweets, nourishing and palatable. — *New York Commercial Advertiser.*

I have only praise for the literary excellence and charm of the book. Lilian Whiting is surely an essayist of exceptional gift ; and the passages of shrewd, worldly wisdom in her writing are often delightfully varied by paragraphs and pages full of the richest human tenderness. — *Edgar Fawcett.*

Lilian Whiting feels the spiritual and intellectual side of life to be of supreme importance, and, what is more, she has the power to make her readers agree with her. Her words raise us from the turmoil and dust of the week's conflict with the business side of life to a higher plane, where are peace and sunshine. It has often seemed to me a remarkable thing that a writer on the daily press should dare to present so constantly this spiritual view of life. Her success in doing so shows that there is a demand for reading of this sort. — *Florence Howe Hall, in a Lecture.*

"The World Beautiful" is a book full of spirituality and optimistic faith, summoning the reader, on every page, to high endeavor and noble, unselfish living, and echoing from title to finis-page the words of St. Paul : "All things work together for good to them that love God ; " "Rejoice alway ; again I say unto you, rejoice."— *The Watchman.*

At all Bookstores. Prepaid, on receipt of price.

ROBERTS BROTHERS, Boston.

EIGHTH THOUSAND.

THE WORLD BEAUTIFUL

(SECOND SERIES).

By LILIAN WHITING,

Author of " The World Beautiful " and "From Dreamland Sent."

16mo. Cloth. Price, $1.00. White and Gold, $1.25.

Rarely does a book appear more rich in thought, suggestive, helpful, practical, unique, and forcible in its lessons for daily life. —*J. W. Chadwick.*

"Kind words and pure thoughts" is the text from which Lilian Whiting delivers some of the best lay sermons ever composed. The thousands of readers who were helped and uplifted in moral tone by THE WORLD BEAUTIFUL, first series, will be glad of this second instalment of essays that are more than essays; which combine a high level of literary achievement with a consecration of purpose and a happiness of style, method, and illustration rarely surpassed. To the weary, be it in well doing or in evil doing, this little volume will come like a reviving draught, instilling courage, inspiration, strength. —*Concord Monitor.*

The book constitutes a noble appeal for higher and more consecrated living. —*Boston Advertiser.*

The second series of essays by Lilian Whiting, collected under the title of THE WORLD BEAUTIFUL, admirably sustains the fine intellectual quality and the ideal of spiritual aspiration which found such graceful expression in a former volume from the same hand. Miss Whiting in this later series dwells at length on the higher possibilities of friendship, and in connection with this theme discusses the determination of social conditions, the art of conversation, the charm of atmosphere, the force of love as a redemptive agency, the virtues of self-control and pleasant speech, and the supreme necessity of an elevated outlook, in adjusting the mind to the experiences of external life. In a concluding chapter the author touches upon the potentialities of the unseen world, and sets forth with contagious earnestness the doctrine that "immortality is a species of conquest in spiritual domain." If, in the course of this discussion, Miss Whiting draws freely upon the occult and the mystic, it must be confessed that she makes effective use of them in the way of pertinent illustration. —*Beacon.*

Sold by all Booksellers. Mailed, postpaid, by Publishers,

ROBERTS BROTHERS, BOSTON.

THIRD EDITION.

From Dreamland Sent.

A Volume of Poems. By Lilian Whiting, author of "The World Beautiful." Cover design by Louise Graves. 16mo. Cloth. Price, $1.25.

Many of Miss Whiting's verses are permeated with the longing, the loneliness, and the wonder of one who looks with chastened heart and seeking eyes after those of her beloved who have passed into the world invisible; but her tears always form prisms for the rainbow of hope, and in her saddest songs there are notes of faith and healing. — *L. A. C.*

This verse gives the keynote of the stanzas throughout the volume. They are replete with poetic feeling and tender sentiment, musical in diction, and chaste in expression. If the feeling comes over us as we read them that they are little more than echoes of grander work, we must admit that they are very sweet echoes, and quite well worth listening to. — *Inter-Ocean.*

The verses have a warmth of feeling in their direct appeal to emotional sympathy that is sure to find a responsive chord in the hearts of all those readers who value poetry, not for its technical perfection, but for the manner in which it voices the joys and sorrows of every-day life and those aspirations which, at favored moments, tend toward the higher ideals of personal conduct. It is rare, indeed, that one comes upon a volume wherein the finer feminine qualities are so artlessly made evident. It has the personal note, and that note is always fine and true. — *The Beacon.*

A dainty little volume of dainty little poems is "From Dreamland Sent," by Lilian Whiting, and worthy the pen of the author of "The World Beautiful." Those who have read her other books and writings will know what to expect in this volume of poems. They are mostly poems of the heart, of love, of sympathy, and affection. Lilian Whiting is by nature a poet, whether she writes in prose or verse, and her verses are flowing and melodious. Repeated expressions of praise are not needed. — *Boston Sunday Times.*

While none of them can be classed among really great poems, yet there is a sweetness and a charm about many of them that will linger in the memory like strains of music. They look on the bright side of life, and are full of hope and faith and courage. — *The Advance.*

Miss Lilian Whiting's poems are notable for the beautiful thoughts which they embody, for the exquisite taste with which these thoughts are treated, and for the sweet expressiveness of the words in which they are dressed. Her verse is like a bit of sunlit landscape on a May morning; it carries one's mind away from stress and turmoil and asserts a suggestion of peace and rest, — not that peace which comes in the evening of life, as the result of work well done, but that peace which stands unperturbed in the midst of struggle, the operation of a quiet mind fixed on permanent things. — *Boston Herald.*

In this little book Lilian Whiting has offered to the world about seventy bits of verse, graceful, tender, and true, appealing to what is best in the human heart. — *Independent.*

These beautiful brief poems, inscribed to Kate Field, all have a meaning and a purpose ; they are artistic in form and finish, full of genuine inspiration. — *Woman's Journal.*

Mailed, postpaid, on receipt of the price, by the publishers,

ROBERTS BROTHERS, Boston.

THE WEDDING GARMENT,

A Tale of the Life to Come.

BY LOUIS PENDLETON.

16mo.   Cloth, price, $1.00.   White and gold, $1.25.

"The Wedding Garment" tells the story of the continued existence of a young man after his death or departure from the natural world. Awakening in the other world, — in an intermediate region between Heaven and Hell, where the good and the evil live together temporarily commingled, — he is astonished and delighted to find himself the same man in all respects as to every characteristic of his mind and ultimate of the body. So closely does everything about him resemble the world he has left behind, that he believes he is still in the latter until convinced of the error. The young man has good impulses, but is no saint, and he listens to the persuasions of certain persons who were his friends in the world, but who are now numbered among the evil, even to the extent of following them downward to the very confines of Hell. Resisting at last and saving himself, later on, and after many remarkable experiences, he gradually makes his way through the intermediate region to the gateways of Heaven, — which can be found only by those prepared to enter, — where he is left with the prospect before him of a blessed eternity in the company of the woman he loves.

The book is written in a reverential spirit, it is unique and quite unlike any story of the same type heretofore published, full of telling incidents and dramatic situations, and not merely a record of the doings of sexless "shades" but of *living* human beings.

The one grand practical lesson which this book teaches, and which is in accord with the divine Word and the New Church unfoldings of it everywhere teach, is the need of an interior, true purpose in life. The deepest ruling purpose which we cherish, what we constantly strive for and determine to pursue as the most real and precious thing of life, that rules us everywhere, that is our ego, our life, is what will have its way at last. It will at last break through all disguise ; it will bring all external conduct into harmony with itself. If it be an evil and selfish end, all external and fair moralties will melt away, and the man will lose his common sense and exhibit his insanities of opinion and will and answering deed on the surface. But if that end be good and innocent, and there be humility within, the outward disorders and evils which result from one's heredity or surroundings will finally disappear. — *From Rev. John Goddard s discourse, July* 1, 1894.

Putting aside the question as to whether the scheme of the soul's development after death was or was not revealed to Swedenborg, whether or not the title of seer can be added to the claims of this learned student of science, all this need not interfere with the moral influence of this work, although the weight of its instruction must be greatly enforced on the minds of those who believe in a later inspiration than the gospels.

This story begins where others end ; the title of the first chapter, "I Die," commands attention; the process of the soul's disenthralment is certainly in harmony with what we sometimes read in the dim eyes of friends we follow to the very gate of life. "By what power does a single spark hold to life so long . . . this lingering of the divine spark of life in a body growing cold?" It is the mission of the author to tear from Death its long-established thoughts of horror, and upon its entrance into a new life, the soul possesses such a power of adjustment that no shock is experienced. — *Boston Transcript.*

ROBERTS BROTHERS, Publishers,

BOSTON. MASS.

THE AIM OF LIFE.

Plain Talks to Young Men and Women.

By Rev. PHILIP STAFFORD MOXOM.

One volume. 16mo. Cloth. 300 pages. Price, $1.00.

Of this book, the *New England Journal of Education* says: "Under the title of THE AIM OF LIFE, Rev. Philip S. Moxom addresses to young people a series of plain, practical talks upon influences that are to be met, contended, or redeemed every day. The essays evince a keen yet sympathetic observation of young manhood and womanhood, and an appreciative regard for its foibles, the force of its environments, and above all, of its possibilities of achievement. That possibility of achievement and the means thereto derives a forceful significance from being made the subject of the first essay and the title of the book. Having thus laid stress on his principle the author forbears to lift up beautiful ideals in the hope that their intrinsic merit shall draw all men unto them, but rather he endeavors to incite the noble instincts that practical every-day life must either foster or annul. Such titles as Character, Companionship, Temperance, Debt, The True Aristocracy, Education, Saving Time, Ethics of Amusement, Reading, Orthodoxy, show the scope of the theme, which if varied in expression, is one throughout all. The essays are not sermonic; they emphasize the power of Christianity; they recognize at the same time the power of personality Christian ethics expressed in plain, forcible language, and innocent of didacticism, young people always appreciate. Such are Dr. Moxom's essays, originally given to the public as addresses to young people in Boston and Cleveland. Now their publication, in convenient form, it is to be hoped, seals their value with permanency."

The Independent says: "Of course it is a good book for young people to read, especially in the view given of character as the supreme result of life."

The Review of Reviews says: "The chapters are marked by a high moral purpose and a direct, vigorous utterance."

The N. Y. Tribune says: "But he presents the old truths in such a vivid and picturesque way, clothing his thoughts, moreover, in such forcible and nervous English, that the most apathetic reader will be stimulated by a perusal of the thirteen chapters that compose the volume."

The Springfield Republican says: "They have a degree of attractiveness quite unusual in volumes of homiletics."

The Outlook says: "The scholar's hand is visible on almost every page, and the way in which etymology is made to yield illustration and exposition of the leading ideas of the successive addresses is both a noticeable literary merit and extremely effective as a method of instruction."

ROBERTS BROTHERS, PUBLISHERS,

BOSTON, MASS.

Dream Life AND Real Life.

𝔄 𝔏𝔦𝔱𝔱𝔩𝔢 𝔄𝔣𝔯𝔦𝔠𝔞𝔫 𝔖𝔱𝔬𝔯𝔶.

By OLIVE SCHREINER,

AUTHOR OF "DREAMS" AND "THE STORY OF AN AFRICAN FARM."

16mo. Half cloth. 60 cents.

These are veritable poems in prose that Olive Schreiner has brought together. With her the theme is ever the martyrdom, the self-sacrifice and the aspirations of woman ; and no writer has expressed these qualities with deeper profundity of pathos or with keener insight into the motives that govern the elemental impulses of the human heart. To read the three little stories in this book is to touch close upon the mysteries of love and fate and to behold the workings of tragedies that are acted in the soul. *The Beacon.*

Three small gems are the only contents of this literary casket ; and yet they reflect so clearly the blending of reality and ideality, and are so perfectly polished with artistic handling, that the reader is quite content with the three. It is a book to be read and enjoyed. — *Public Opinion.*

There is a peculiar charm about all of these stories that quite escapes the cursory reader. It is as evasive as the fragrance of the violet, and equally difficult to analyze. The philosophy is so subtle, the poetry so delicate, that the fascination grows upon one and defies description. With style that is well nigh classic in its simplicity Miss Schreiner excites our emotions and gently stimulates our imagination. — *The Budget.*

All the sketches reveal originality of treatment, but the first one is a characteristically pathetic reproduction of child-life under exceptional circumstances, that will bring tears to many eyes. — *Saturday Evening Gazette.*

Sold by all booksellers. Mailed, post-paid, on receipt of the price by the Publishers.

ROBERTS BROTHERS, Boston.

LIFE IN HEAVEN.

THERE, FAITH IS CHANGED INTO SIGHT, AND HOPE IS PASSED INTO BLISSFUL FRUITION.

A New Work by the Author of "Heaven our Home," and "Meet for Heaven."

16mo. Cloth. Price, $1.00.

———◆———

In the same beautiful style with the series we have noticed, both of composition and of external finish. The chapters are not doctrinal disquisitions. The doctrine is indeed the basis; but the superstructure is contemplation. Heaven is a blissful world, as a goal to which we travel; the joys of the arrival, the glorious society attained, and the blessed intercourse in the heavenly home, are the prevailing topics of the book. They are presented in a pure, vivid, realizing style. They open before us those vistas revealed to us in the blessed word, enabling us to feel that there is a great result for which to live and labor. — *Methodist Quarterly Review.*

The dangerous delusion that we shall be totally changed in heaven is forcibly opposed. We must take our characters here for all eternity, he teaches. The book is a good addition to a religious library. — *Hartford Press.*

The mind and heart never weary of the effort to pierce the veil which separates us from the dear dead, and to learn how they fare in the spirit world. The author of these works appears to have ministered to this craving, not in an imaginative and speculative way, but in one that is practical, and which keeps close to the testimony. His previous works on these subjects have been well received; and this volume will be found of equal interest. — *Episcopal Recorder.*

Few writers have done more in the way of portraying heaven, its enjoyments and employments, than the author of this work. Few have done more to direct the mind of the Christian to the great work of preparation for the enjoyment of heaven than he. Those who have read his "Meet for Heaven" and "Heaven our Home" will peruse this work with special pleasure. — *Pittsburgh Witness.*

———◆———

Sold by all Booksellers. Mailed, postpaid, on receipt of price, by the Publishers,

ROBERTS BROTHERS, Boston.

HEAVEN OUR HOME.

WE HAVE NO SAVIOUR BUT JESUS, AND NO HOME BUT HEAVEN.

BY THE AUTHOR OF "MEET FOR HEAVEN," AND "LIFE IN HEAVEN."

16mo. Cloth. Price, $1.00.

In boldness of conception, startling minuteness of delineation, and originality of illustration, this work, by an anonymous author, exceeds any of the kind we have ever read. — *John O'Groat Journal.*

The name of the author of this work is strangely enough withheld. A social heaven, in which there will be the most perfect recognition, intercourse, fellowship and bliss, is the leading idea of the book; and it is discussed in a fine, genial spirit. — *Caledonian Mercury.*

I wish that every Christian person could have the perusal of these writings. I can never be sufficiently thankful to him who wrote them for the service he has rendered to me and all others.

They have given *form and substance to everything revealed in the Scriptures respecting our heavenly home of love*, and they have done not a little to invest it with the most powerful attractions to my heart. Since I have enjoyed the privilege of following the thought of their author, I have felt that there was a *reality* in all these things which I have never felt before; and I find myself often thanking God for putting it into the heart of a poor worm of the dust to spread such glorious representations before our race, all of whom stand in need of such a rest. — *Rev. Samuel L. Tuttle, Assistant Secretary of the American Bible Society.*

Every one will say when he lays down this book, "I never knew there was so much said in the Bible about heaven."

The soul seems to loosen from the clay and depart, and when we find at the close of the volume that he is still in the earth, like Paul, he desires "to depart and be with Christ, which is far better." The other two works of the "Heaven Series," entitled "Meet for Heaven" and "Life in Heaven," are just as full and as entirely interesting as the one under notice. They form the most important works of the kind that have ever been published or reported in the United States.

To the old, they have not that eulogistic praise of the world that Rendel's work possesses; the middle-aged will say to the wheels of time, Roll faster;

> "Speed me to my home
> Where God and angels are."

The young will find them telling of the prize at the end of the race, and their feet will be stayed on God. The dying will bless the writer for the reality of anticipated visions. — *Christian Advocate, Richmond.*

Sold by all Booksellers. Mailed, postpaid, on receipt of price, by the Publishers,

ROBERTS BROTHERS, BOSTON.

STORIES OF THE SEEN AND THE UNSEEN.

BY

Mrs. MARGARET O. W. OLIPHANT.

This volume includes the four books hitherto published anonymously, viz.: "A Little Pilgrim: In the Unseen;" "The Little Pilgrim: Further Experiences, etc.;" "Old Lady Mary, a Story of the Seen and the Unseen;" "The Open Door. The Portrait: Two Stories of the Seen and the Unseen."

One volume. 16mo. Cloth. Price, $1.25.

———◆———

As bits of imaginative writing, Mrs. Oliphant's "Stories of the Seen and the Unseen" are exquisite productions. The experience of the Little Pilgrim on her waking in heaven, and her return to earth with her soul filled with the light of a Divine beneficence and her mind sure of those higher truths, to soothe earthly sufferers revolting against the bitterness of loss and pain, are told with the sublimated spirituality of one who has just passed through a long illness, and whose mind, weak to the impressions of the external world, is peculiarly sensitive to spiritual visions. No one could have written with more poetic delicacy of the subjective and objective blessedness of that state of future existence which the human heart pictures to itself by the word heaven; and the story of "Old Lady Mary" will remain a distinct success among tales of imaginative literature. — *The Critic.*

We commend the literary delicacy and power of these stories, and even more their tender, stimulating spirituality. — *Congregationalist.*

Deep spiritual truths are given a new beauty; the idea of Divine love and beneficence is never lost sight of, and the heart that is filled with sorrow will find in the story of the Little Pilgrim a soothing charm and a something that may heal the scars which have been made by grief and bereavement. — *Philadelphia Record.*

———◆———

For sale by all booksellers. Mailed, post-paid, on receipt of price, by the publishers,

ROBERTS BROTHERS, Boston.

MARY W. TILESTON'S SELECTIONS.

Daily Strength for Daily Needs. Selections for every day
in the year. 16mo. Plain $1.00
THE SAME. White, gilt 1.25
" " Padded calf 3.50
" " " mor. 3.00
Sunshine in the Soul. Poems of Encouragement and Cheer-
fulness. 16mo. Plain 1.00
THE SAME. White, gilt 1.25
" " Padded calf 3.50
" " " mor. 3.00
First and Second Series, separately 50
Quiet Hours. A Collection of Poems. Square 16mo. First
and Second Series, each 1.00
THE SAME. Two volumes in one. 16mo 1.50
" " White gilt 1.75
" " Flexible mor. 3.50
Sursum Corda. Hymns of Comfort. 16mo 1.25
The Blessed Life. Favorite Hymns. Square 18mo 1.00
Classic Heroic Ballads. 16mo. 1.00

WISDOM SERIES.

*Issued in handsome pocket volumes. 18mo. Flexible covers,
red edges.*

Selections from the Apocrypha $0.50
**The Wisdom of Jesus, the Son of Sirach ; or, Ecclesias-
ticus** 50
**Selections from the Thoughts of Marcus Aurelius
Antoninus** 50
THE SAME. Mor., $1.50; calf 2.50
Selections from the Imitation of Christ 50
Selections from Epictetus 50
THE SAME. Mor., $1.50; calf 2.50
Selections from the Life and Sermons of Tauler . . .50
Selections from Fénelon. 50
THE SAME. Mor., $1.50; calf 2.50
Socrates. The Apology and Crito of Plato 50
Socrates. The Phædo of Plato 50

Sold by all booksellers. Mailed, postpaid, on receipt of price.

ROBERTS BROTHERS, BOSTON.

DAILY STRENGTH FOR DAILY NEEDS.

SELECTED BY THE EDITOR OF "QUIET HOURS."

16mo. Cloth, Price $1.00; white cloth, gilt, $1.25.

———◆———

"This little book is made up of selections from Scripture, and verses of poetry, and prose selections for each day of the year. We turn with confidence to any selections of this kind which Mrs. Tileston may make. In her 'Quiet Hours,' 'Sunshine for the Soul,' 'The Blessed Life,' and other works, she has brought together a large amount of rich devotional material in a poetic form. Her present book does not disappoint us. We hail with satisfaction every contribution to devotional literature which shall be acceptable to liberal Christians. This selection is made up from a wide range of authors, and there is an equally wide range of topics. It is an excellent book for private devotion or for use at the family altar." — *Christian Register.*

"It is made up of brief selections in prose and verse, with accompanying texts of Scripture, for every day in the year, arranged by the editor of 'Quiet Hours,' and for the purpose of 'bringing the reader to perform the duties and to bear the burdens of each day with cheerfulness and courage.' It is hardly necessary to say that the selection is admirably made, and that the names one finds scattered through the volume suggest the truest spiritual insight and aspiration. It is a book to have always on one's table, and to make one's daily companion." — *Christian Union.*

"They are the words of those wise and holy men, who, in all ages have realized the full beauty of spiritual experience. They are words to comfort, to encourage, to strengthen, and to uplift into faith and aspiration. It is pleasant to think of the high and extended moral development that were possible, if such a book were generally the daily companion and counsellor of thinking men and women. Every day of the year has its appropriate text and appropriate thoughts, all helping towards the best life of the reader. Such a volume needs no appeal to gain attention to it." — *Sunday Globe, Boston.*

————

Sold by all booksellers. Mailed, post-paid, on receipt of price, by the Publishers,

ROBERTS BROTHERS. BOSTON

www.ingramcontent.com/pod-product-compliance
Lightning Source LLC
Chambersburg PA
CBHW031107020726
47495CB00007B/2084